Summer TEMPTATION

Summer Temptation

WENDY S. MARCUS

Summary Temptation – The Hot in the Hamptons Series

Cover Design by: Billington Media
Editor: Gena Lopata
Formatted by: Tianne Samson with E.M. Tippetts Book Designs

emtippettsbookdesigns.com

Dear Reader,

Come play in the Hamptons sandbox with the Hot in the Hamptons series, a trilogy featuring SUMMER DREAMING (Liz Matis), SUMMER TEMPTATION (Wendy S. Marcus), and SUMMER SINS (Jennifer Probst). Three separate novellas. Three different authors. One summer to remember.

Read them all, or just read one. It's up to you! But when read together you'll find extra story scenes to enhance your reading pleasure. No matter which route you choose, these standalone novellas will make you burn.

Books By
WENDY S. MARCUS

Random House Loveswept
Contemporary Romance:

All I Need Is You (Loving You #2) Coming October 6, 2015
Loving You Is Easy (Loving You #1)

COSMOPOLITAN Red-Hot Reads from Harlequin:
The V-Spot

Harlequin Medical Romance:
Tempting Nurse Scarlet
Secrets of a Shy Socialite
Craving Her Soldier's Touch
A Nurse's Not So Secret Scandal
Once a Good Girl
When One Night Isn't Enough

Acknowledgements

A special thank you to Liz Matis for suggesting the three of us should do a series together. Another special thank you to Jennifer Probst who offered up her beautiful home and served us lunch when we met up to put the finishing touches on our stories. I couldn't have asked for better writing partners. Thank you both for your patience in answering all of my questions. The next time we get together, drinks are on me!!!

Chapter One

Leigh DeGray

Being fresh out of college, about to start your dream job, and winding up pregnant isn't the end of the world, I told myself, again, as I slowed down to avoid rear-ending the car in front of me. I'd survived worse, like losing my mom and older brother in a tragic car accident when I was only twelve years old. Like almost losing Grandpa Carl, who was like a second father to me, after he'd suffered a stroke three months ago and almost losing my dad, the most important person in my world, to a heart attack a few weeks after that.

I could survive being pregnant at the age of twenty-one.

I could raise a child on my own.

If it turned out I was, in fact, pregnant.

Technically, at the moment, I was only late…going on six weeks late, the tardiness of my period unprecedented since my entrance into womanhood. The last few months had been crazy hectic and stressful which surely explained my current… irregularity.

I mean, in addition to dealing with dad's and grandpa's health crises, I'd successfully presented final projects and aced final exams to graduate summa cum laude from Penn State. After sending out twenty-nine resumés and attending twenty-seven job interviews in five different states over the past six weeks, I'd landed a coveted position in the NYC office of Hollis and Hamilton, the largest and most prestigious public relations firm in the country.

Anyone's system would be a little messed up after all that.

I glanced in my side mirror, then over my shoulder, before steering into the left lane to pass a truck, wondering how my employer would react to finding out the one new hire they'd allotted themselves, who they'd chosen from hundreds of applicants, was pregnant. Rather than working long hours and jetting across the country at a moment's notice, I would soon need time off for doctors' appointments, maternity leave, and childcare issues. The thought of that conversation sat heavy in my gut – for sure the reason I suddenly felt queasy and in desperate need to escape my car.

Lucky me, I noticed a cute little restaurant coming up on the left, so I slowed down, clicked on my signal, and pulled into the turning lane. Then I sat and watched the oncoming cars, inching along, bumper to bumper. Gotta love summer traffic in the Hamptons. Not!

Finally a nice woman let me go, and I squeezed my dependable Subaru Outback into an opening that I'm not sure was an actual parking spot, but who could tell in a gravel lot? My head resting back, eyes closed, I fumbled for the button to open my window and breathed in the warm summer air tinged with the scent of the ocean. This was exactly what I needed: rest and relaxation, the beach, fun in the sun with my two best friends from college, Storme and Kelsey. Our last hurrah before we embarked on life as responsible adults.

A delicious charbroil smell wafted past my window, and suddenly I was hungrier than I could ever remember being. I glanced at the clock. No wonder! Almost four in the afternoon, and I hadn't eaten since breakfast. I grabbed my phone to text Storme.

Starving. Stopped to eat. Will be there before the pool party. Promise.

Then I threw the phone into my pocketbook and headed inside.

Of course I didn't have a reservation, so of course there were no tables available on the pretty outdoor terrace or in the crowded indoor dining room. I opted for the last remaining seat at the far end of the bar.

"Just a glass of water with lemon," I told the bartender, though I really wanted an over-sized wineglass filled to the rim with cabernet. "And a menu."

He smiled at me, that 'hey baby, what's a pretty girl like you doing here all alone?' kind of smile. I'm used to it. Not to be conceited, but I've been blessed with a clear complexion, my dad's green eyes, and mom's trim figure, that I don't really remember but I've seen in pictures. I lowered my eyes and gave him my demure half-smile. Move along, buddy. Good girl here. Well, at least most of the time.

Under the guise of checking my phone for messages, I secretly snuck glimpses of my fellow bar patrons, my eyes lingering on an older gentleman, mid-seventies, sitting catty-corner to me on the right, his head down, shoulders slumped, so sad. A rock glass filled with some amber-colored liquid sat on the bar in front of him, untouched. He pulled a white linen handkerchief, same as my grandpa always used to carry, from a pocket in his red-knit sweater vest, lifted it to blot an eye, and I had to ask, "Sir?" I reached out and placed my hand on his white dress shirt covered forearm. "Are you okay?"

He looked up and my heart broke at the sight of tears in his kind gray-blue eyes.

He cleared his throat. "Me? I'm fine." He tucked the handkerchief back in his pocket. "Just fine." Then he stared at his drink, lifted it, and took a sip.

Okay then. At least I'd tried.

When the bartender returned with my water and a menu, I gave him a quick, "Thank you," and went in search of my hamburger options. My mouth watered, remembering the enticing charbroil smell that'd drawn me inside.

The older gentleman spoke. I lifted my head and found him looking at me. "I'm sorry," I said, closing the menu. "What did you say?"

"Today would have been my fiftieth wedding anniversary."

Would have been.

"Proposed to my wife right out there on the porch." He

motioned to the window with his hand.

A beautiful spot overlooking the ocean. So romantic.

"This place has changed owners over the years, but we come back on this date, every year, to celebrate. The kids talked about having a big party...but my Lilly couldn't hold on. A stroke took her from me. Three months ago."

Darn strokes. Evil things. My heart ached for his loss as well as for my own. Even though my grandpa had survived *his* stroke, he could no longer communicate or take care of himself. And he no longer recognized his family. In my mind, maybe death would have been easier to deal with. "I'm so sorry."

"And here I am." He looked down at his drink. "Didn't know where else to go." He lifted his sad eyes to mine. "It seemed like a good idea yesterday, when I made the reservation, but now... I don't want to be here alone."

This sweet old man reminded me of my grandpa: same glasses, same white hair, and the same quiet, gentle manner.

Just then the hostess came over, holding a menu. "Mr. Kenzy. Your table is ready."

"I, uh..." He slid off the chair clumsily, like he'd stiffened up during the time he'd been sitting. I hurried off my own stool to steady him. "I don't think..." He hesitated.

An idea popped into my head, something that would, perhaps, cheer us both. "Would you give us a moment?" I asked the hostess. At her nod, I turned to my new friend. "I don't have any pressing plans." Storme and Kelsey might disagree, but this was something I had to do. "I know it's forward of me, but I'd be honored to join you for dinner, so you wouldn't have to eat alone. I'm happy to listen to stories about your wife, if you feel up to sharing them, to celebrate her life and your almost fifty years together. You don't have to pay for me, I'll —"

"No plans? You?" He looked me up and down, his expression a total ego boost. "On a Friday night? What is with young men today? A bunch of idiots." He shook his head in disgust.

I smiled. He was absolutely adorable.

Holding his arm out in front of him, bent at the elbow, same as my grandpa used to do, he said, "My name's Murphy. Would you care to dine with me on this fine afternoon?"

I slid my hand into the crook of his arm. "I'm Leigh. And I'd be honored."

Murphy told the hostess, "I'm ready now." He glanced over at me with a smile. "And it seems my table for one has turned into a table for two."

"Certainly, sir," she said with a courteous smile. Then she led us outside to a lovely table on the patio overlooking the Atlantic Ocean.

The food delicious, the company enjoyable, and the view fantastic, the evening ranked up there with the top ten best dinner dates I'd ever had…until a younger, taller, much handsomer version of Murphy approached our table.

And he didn't look at all happy.

Chapter Two

Nick Kenzy

Un-fucking-believable. After the overwhelmingly shitty day I'd had, plus fighting the late day summer commute, on a Friday no less, to get to my grandfather's house in the Hamptons – and pounding on the door, almost to the point of panic, before checking the garage to see the car he rarely drove anymore, missing, he'd gone to the restaurant, after I'd specifically told him not to. My heart pounding, a mixture of stress, anger, and relief surging through my veins, I approached his table, recognizing the back of his favorite red sweater vest immediately. It wasn't until I was a few feet away that I realized he wasn't alone.

What the hell? I stopped mid-stride, ducking to the side, watching without being seen, unable to believe my tired eyes. Right there in front of me, a mere few feet away, sat my grieving granddad, across from a stunning woman, who looked to be younger than his youngest grandson, which would be me, smiling.

Her light-brownish-reddish hair fell over bare, porcelain-colored shoulders. She wore a simple sundress made of some colorful, shimmery fabric. It didn't cling to her breasts, didn't expose her cleavage, yet on her it looked sexy and alluring and…she was on a date with my grandfather, a man at least fifty-years her senior.

Why?

Who was she?

I continued forward, coming to a stop beside him. "Murphy." I ignored his dinner guest. For now. "I told you to wait for me." I didn't like him driving in the summer traffic.

He removed his napkin from his lap and blotted some steak sauce from his lips guiltily, wiping away the evidence. Like I couldn't tell by what remained on his plate that he'd eaten a steak, even though his doctor had told him no more red meat. "But my reservation was for four o'clock. It's the only one I could get. You said you couldn't make it that early."

Because I had a job; at least, I'd had one during our conversation yesterday. God I needed a drink. "I told you I'd get out here as soon as I could. That we'd go to a different restaurant."

"But I wanted to come here. We *always* come here. Your grandmother loves this place."

Loves, present tense, not loved, past tense. Had Murphy lost his mind? "Grandma's dead." The fact that she loved this restaurant no longer mattered.

Grandpa's dinner companion sucked in an affronted breath.

Shit. I must have said that out loud.

While I didn't know the woman and could have cared less what she thought of me, the hurt in my granddad's eyes made me apologize. "I'm sorry." The last thing I wanted to do was hurt his feelings, especially knowing how difficult today must be for him. "I didn't mean…"

Angry, unfamiliar yet mesmerizing green eyes stared up at me. "Of all the insensitive…"

I stopped listening, her straight white teeth and perfectly shaped pink lips distracting me.

"…should be ashamed of yourself," she finished up, her voice pleasing, if not for the scolding tone. And that scolding tone rubbed me the wrong way. Who the hell did this stranger think she was? She didn't know me. Didn't know the day I'd had. Didn't know my granddad. Hadn't been dealing with his broken heart, declining health, and diminishing eyesight, all while trying to keep a demanding job in New York City that comfortably supported us both.

A job I no longer had. I squeezed my eyes shut and pinched the bridge of my nose to keep my head from exploding. I inhaled, exhaled, and then focused on the stranger judging me. "And who might you be?" I'd tried for a congenial tone. I'd failed.

"This is Leigh," granddad answered for her, as if the name 'Leigh' should mean something to me. As if he'd ever mentioned the name 'Leigh' before — he hadn't, I would have remembered. As if by simply stating her name I would have all of the answers to all of my questions. *Who the hell is she? Why is she here?*

"How do you know Leigh?" I asked, seething.

"We met in the bar."

I watched her, sitting quietly, so beautiful and sexy, like she had every right to be there. Well, she didn't. Nice clothes. She had money. Perfectly put together in a very appealing package. Then it hit me. I knew exactly who Leigh was, and I wanted to strangle her for preying on a heartbroken, lonely old man.

"Damn it, Murphy." I felt my tie squeezing my throat, so I yanked it off. "Can't you see what she is?"

Grandpa looked Leigh over, confused, trying to see what I saw.

"A prostitute," I said, probably louder than I should have. Someone dropped a piece of silverware on their plate. Someone close by gasped, probably a female, but I couldn't be certain. Conversation quieted down as people in our general vicinity turned their attention to us.

I didn't give a crap. I hadn't eaten since breakfast. My head throbbed, my blood pressure had to be approaching stroke range, and I had reached my limit of bullshit for the day.

Granddad shook his head. "No."

"Why else do you think a young, beautiful woman would pick you up in a bar?" I asked, exhausted and needing to sit down.

Leigh shot to her feet. "Because he looked sad and lonely," she snapped, balling up her napkin and throwing it down on the table. "Because he told me today would have been his fiftieth wedding anniversary, only his beautiful Lilly couldn't hold on to celebrate it. I offered to help him celebrate their life together and honor her memory on this very special day because he was here all alone." She glared at me then, turned, and yanked her purse from the back of her chair. "And because he reminds me of my own grandpa, who I've been missing very much."

She wiped an eye.

Fuck. Me. Either this Leigh was an Academy Award winning actress I'd never heard of, or she was telling the truth.

She reached into her purse, took out her wallet, and threw two twenty-dollar bills down on the table.

"My treat," Murphy stood and handed her back her money.

She shook her head, refusing to take it.

He shot me his 'I'll deal with you later' look, then pushed me aside so he could draw Leigh into a hug. "I gave you my phone number," he said, patting her back. "Whenever you're missing your grandpa, you give me a call, okay?"

She sniffled. "Thank you, Murphy. I will."

I could almost feel the scorn of people sitting around me for the way I'd misread the situation. That's it. I was done. Too tired to apologize, too tired to care, too tired to deal with one more fucking thing today, I plopped into my granddad's chair.

The waiter joined the party. "Is everything okay over here?" he asked, eyeing Leigh like a puppy in love before shooting me a nonverbal 'You're an asshole.'

I pointed to granddad's rock glass. "I'll have what he's having. Make it a double. No ice." And please, don't spit in it.

Without a glance my way, Leigh gave my granddad a sweet kiss on the cheek, said her goodbye, and left, as beautiful from the back as she was from the front: classy, composed, and too well-mannered to call me a fucking idiot.

"You're a fucking idiot, you know that?" Granddad said,

sitting down across from me in the seat Leigh had just vacated, watching me as I watched her leave.

If I'd had the energy, I would have pointed out he never would have spoken like that when grandma was alive. In fact, his use of profanity seemed to be on the upswing lately. Maybe I should mention that to the doctor at his next appointment.

"She's really something, isn't she?" he said, his tone softening. "Reminds me of my Lilly when we first met." His tone took on a dreamy quality, as if remembering the day. Then he smiled. "I can sure pick em' can't I? Your granddad's still got it."

That smile, again, when I hadn't seen it in months…and he was smiling because of Leigh.

My drink came and I chugged it down. Then Murphy insisted I eat something before he'd let me drive. While I scarfed down a cheeseburger and fries, he ate a piece of the chocolate layer cake he and grandma used to share on their anniversary while he spoke at length about his earlier dinner companion.

"She's staying with a friend in Wainscott, over in East Hampton."

Probably with her boyfriend, who no doubt had more money than I did.

"You owe her an apology, you know." He used his napkin to wipe some chocolate icing from his upper lip.

Maybe I did. "How do you propose I go about doing that? Do you have her telephone number?"

"No." He shook his head. "I only gave her mine."

"Do you know where she's staying in Wainscott?"

He shook his head again. Then his eyes widened. "But

she did mention she and her friends are going to a big bonfire Sunday night." He smiled. "I bet you could find out where."

Shit.

Chapter Three

Leigh

It took another forty-five minutes in the car, more because of traffic than distance, to get to Storme's beach house. I made good use of my time to calm down after that awful confrontation with Murphy's horrible grandson. Poor Murphy, having to deal with that rude, controlling halfwit on a regular basis.

Too bad his short dark hair, sensual blue eyes, and brooding good looks were wasted on a tall, well-put-together man who was completely lacking in manners, tact, and personality.

Feeling much more relaxed, I pulled into Storme's driveway. The house…took my breath away. Opulent came to mind. Huge. More of an estate than the 'summer cottage' she'd invited me to visit. For fun and frolic, she'd said. Honestly, I wasn't the type to frolic, but fun? I was in dire need of some fun.

I parked my trusty, six-year-old white Subaru right between Storme's shiny, cherry red convertible and the dark blue, classic muscle car Kelsey had inherited from her dad when she'd turned twenty-one. I think she'd called it a 1968 Shelby Mustang, as if that meant something. The cars, like the three of us, couldn't be more different.

Storme, a gorgeous brunette, Kelsey, a beautiful blond, as strong as she was pretty, and me, with light brownish-red hair and okay looks, at least in my opinion. Storme's family very wealthy and living life so everybody knew it, Kelsey's family the exact opposite of wealthy, and my family…well, my dad made a lot of money, but we lived our lives somewhere in between.

The front door opened and Storme ran out first, her dark wavy hair loose, wearing skimpy denim shorts and a clingy pink tank top. "Finally. If you didn't get here soon we were going to go out looking for you." She pulled me into a hug.

Kelsey followed behind her, blond hair up in a loose, messy knot, dressed in 'thrift shop chic,' as she called it, but always managing to look great. "Heard you tried to back out," she said, her words tinged with a sweet southern accent as she hugged me too. "We would have come up to Westchester to get you." She looked me in the eyes. "You know that, right?"

I smiled, deciding I'd wait until later to tell them my plans to return home at least one night a week to check on my dad and grandpa. "Why else do you think I came?"

"To spend the summer in the Hamptons," Storme said. "To relax on the beach during the day and party all night."

Threat of sunburn aside, relaxing on the beach sounded great. Partying all night? Not so much.

"To meet hot guys and have raunchy sex under the starry sky." Kelsey winked.

She knew that wasn't me at all.

"Stop it," Storme said, giving Kelsey a playful push on the shoulder. Then she slid her arm through mine and led me up the stairs and into the house. "I'd settle for Leigh meeting one nice guy for a sweet summer romance." Storme glanced up at me. "Before you lose yourself in sixty hour work weeks and coast to coast travel."

Storme guided me though an exquisite entryway with immaculate white walls, along beautiful dark hardwood floors, to a huge open kitchen toward the back of the house.

"Yeah," Kelsey said, pouring a glass of white wine and handing it to me. "We're not going to be there to pull you out of the library and force you to have a social life."

To be honest, that worried me a little bit.

I took the glass. If I'd refused, my friends would have known something was wrong, because I love my wine. I took a sip. Certainly a few small sips wouldn't hurt the baby…if there was a baby.

"What's wrong?" Storme asked. She could read me better than anyone.

"Nothing," I lied, pulling up a chair to take a seat at the counter.

She gave me that worried look that usually got me talking, but not this time. I would not bring down the happy vibe in the room or take the focus away from our summer of carefree fun and planning for Storme's end-of-summer wedding by sharing my pregnancy concern.

And that, in a nutshell, was why I hadn't taken a pregnancy test. If I didn't know for certain, then I could cling to the hope I wasn't pregnant, that the future I'd planned so carefully was not on the verge of falling apart, that I wouldn't be responsible for finishing off my dad with the news he was about to become a grandpa. No downward spiral of doom and gloom necessary.

I looked up. Great, Kelsey had concern in her eyes, too. Knowing I had to give them something to explain my sudden quiet, I swirled my glass and took another small sip. "Every time I drink this I'll think of both of you and how much you mean to me."

'This,' of course, being the delicious wine produced by Storme's family's vineyard, right on Long Island.

"I'd say the same," Kelsey took a sip from her own glass, "except this stuff is too expensive for my budget."

"Once you figure out what you'll be doing after the summer, and where you'll be doing it, I'll have a case delivered to you every month," Storme said, like it was no big deal, because to her, it wasn't. Sure, she loved her designer clothes and fancy cars, but other than that, there was nothing 'rich girl' about Storme. She was the kindest, sweetest, most generous person I'd ever met.

"To friendship." I held up my glass in a toast. "Rooming with the two of you freshman year was the best thing that ever happened to me." Storme, the outgoing life of the party, Kelsey fun but more selective in her friends, and me, the quiet one, happier alone with my Kindle than out at a party or bar. Yet somehow we'd bonded like sisters that year, and our friendship had only grown stronger since then.

We all clinked glasses.

"To getting Leigh laid," Kelsey said.

"I'll drink to that." Storme tapped her glass to Kelsey's.

Since the last time I'd 'gotten laid' – or gotten close to getting laid — may not have worked out so well for me, I tried to interrupt. "Hey, wait a minute." But they both leaned in and tapped my glass with big smiles on their faces.

Storme added, "And to Kelsey finally fulfilling her lifeguard fantasy."

Kelsey laughed. "I am all over that."

I hoped, with all my heart, that Kelsey *did* meet a big, strong, sexy lifeguard for the summer fling she'd been talking about for months. She was such a loyal friend, always there for me. After losing her dad in the war, if anyone deserved a little happiness in her life, Kelsey did.

"And to Storme having the perfect wedding," I said, holding out my glass. Was it my imagination, or did the soon-to-be bride hesitate before clinking my glass? Did her smile falter? Was that uncertainty I saw flash in her eyes?

If so, she recovered quickly, raising her glass. "Of course I will. I have the two best maids-of-honor ever who will make sure I do."

"You know it," Kelsey said.

"Of course," I agreed, watching my friend, wondering what was going on in that head of hers.

After that we sat around for a while talking about what we'd been doing since graduation. I gave them updates on dad and grandpa. Storme filled us in on some new wedding plans, and Kelsey talked about possibly going to Europe for graduate school and the lifeguard she'd met earlier that day.

All too soon Storme insisted on showing me to my room, which had a private bathroom attached, so we could get changed for a pool party I had no desire to go to.

Chapter Four

Nick

When had I gotten so old? When was the last time I'd walked on the beach? I missed the feel of sand between my toes, so I kicked off my flip flops and carried them. I missed the smell of the ocean and the sound of waves crashing into the shore, so I took a moment to enjoy the beauty of the sun setting over the water. As much as I hadn't wanted to come tonight, the bonfire up ahead, the music, and the laughter had me feeling a bit nostalgic for the summers of my youth, when my life revolved around lifeguarding and pretty girls in tiny bikinis.

Two years of eighty hour work weeks as an analyst on Wall Street, and at the age of twenty-four I felt closer to forty. Forget fun. At present, my social life consisted of networking with business associates, always looking to get noticed, always fighting for that promotion, and not much else.

For the past year, my downtime, what little I had, had all been spent with grandma and granddad, doing the things my parents should have been doing, only they'd chosen North Carolina over Long Island. To escape the New York winters, they'd said initially. Now they stayed down there year round.

"Nick! My man! How's it going?"

"Jake." I held out my pasty white hand to shake my old friend's sunbaked, golden brown one.

Nothing escaped Jake. He held up my hand, squinting at the imagined glare from my skin. "That office job is killing you," he said. "Sucking the color of life right out of you."

No argument there. "I'll be sticking around for a few days." Not by choice, more like for lack of anything better to do while I updated my resumé and got in touch with a few headhunters to get my job search going. "Should have my color back in no time."

At the thought of kicking around the beach, doing some swimming and bikini watching, my spirits lifted. "Where you hiding the beer?" Despite the restriction on alcohol, I knew the big red plastic cups everyone had were not filled with soda.

Jake pointed to an Italian ice pushcart. "Keg's in there."

I smiled. "Like old times."

"You know it." Jake held out his fist and I bumped it with mine. "Now get yourself a nice cold drink, shake off that New York City grime, and let's have us some fun."

Just what I needed.

It didn't take long to find Leigh. All I had to do was look in the direction most of the men around me kept looking, and there she was with her two friends. Each one dressed in a similar, colorful beach cover-up that left one shoulder and their long, slender legs bare. Each one was as pretty as the next: a blond, a brunette, and a light-brownish-redhead, one for each preference.

If only the light-brownish-redhead didn't think I was a total ass.

Leigh separated from her friends and walked toward a large plastic trash barrel over by a set of wooden stairs. She looked around as if trying to see if her friends were watching. They weren't, but I was, and I saw her dump the contents of her big red plastic cup into the barrel, take a bottle of water from her string backpack, and pour its contents into the cup before tossing away the container.

Interesting.

Apparently seeing Leigh on her own, vulnerable prey separated from the herd, a big guy, more bulk than brawn, staggered in her direction. I headed that way, too. Just in case. When he reached her, Leigh smiled politely and tried to walk around him. He stopped her. I picked up my pace.

Before I could get there, Leigh's blond friend jogged over. A few quick words I couldn't hear, and the guy turned himself right back around.

Leigh laughed. A beautiful sound. Then she smiled. For some reason, that smile warmed my insides. On the way back to their brunette friend, Leigh stopped and pulled a cell phone out of her bag to take a call. Motioning toward the water, her blond friend nodded, and Leigh walked off on her own.

Naturally, I followed. To keep her safe, I told myself, feeling rather protective of the woman who'd shown my granddad such kindness. The woman who'd made him happier than I'd seen him in months. The woman who'd impressed him so much he could hardly stop talking about her – to the point I felt like I knew her.

The fact that I liked following her, watching her graceful form as she walked, pretty painted toenails, toned legs, and hips swaying… Well, that was an added bonus.

Except I started to feel a bit like a creeper, stalking along after her.

When she settled into a spot on the sand, facing the ocean, the waves almost reaching the tips of her toes before receding, I returned to the fringes of the party, giving her privacy, still on guard, waiting for my chance to talk to her so I could apologize.

"Hey there, handsome." A young woman with black hair piled into a loose, messy bun on top of her head walked over to me, smiling. "You look lonely."

I wasn't.

She held out her hand. "I'm Mackenzie."

Good manners had me reaching out to shake it. "Nick."

"You from around here?" she asked. "Or just visiting for the summer?"

Mackenzie made conversation easy, asking lots of questions, pretending to be interested in me and my life. There was a time I would have jumped at the chance to pick up a woman like her. She was pretty enough, with a bangin' body and flirty personality, but tonight…tonight she didn't do anything for me.

What the…? "I've gotta run," I told her and left without waiting for a response, because at some point in the last few minutes, some guy had planted his butt in the sand next to Leigh. I didn't like that one bit.

"Leigh," I yelled as I approached. In the fading light, she turned toward me, then disentangled herself from the arm wrapped around her shoulders and stood. Relieved? Angry? I couldn't tell. Not welcoming, that was for sure.

"What are *you* doing here?"

"Dude, keep moving," the guy beside her said, as he stood too. "I got here first."

As if that gave him the right to have her.

Leigh dropped her phone into her string backpack, slung it over her shoulders and crossed her arms over her chest.

"Let me guess," she said to me. "Your grandfather made you track me down to apologize."

Yup. She knew it, and I knew it, so why lie? As soon as she gave the guy standing next to her the kiss off, I could get it over with and be on my way.

But she didn't give him the kiss off. Instead, she stood there, looking back and forth between the two of us.

"What?" I asked. "Am I interrupting? Did you *want* this guy's attention?"

"Actually," she said. "I'm trying to decide which of you is the lesser of two evils."

I couldn't help it. I smiled. It felt good.

"Pick me, babe," the surfer dude said, raising his hand. "You want evil? I'm up for anything. Let me take you back to my place and show you."

His brain likely fried from a mix of sun and marijuana, he'd totally missed her point. That made me smile even more.

Leigh rolled her eyes. "Well that makes my decision easier." She took a giant step toward me. "Sorry, Big One."

"Your loss," he said with a shrug. Then he strutted back to the party, likely in search of another babe to take back to his place.

"Big One?" I asked.

"He said people call him that for *lots* of reasons." She glanced up at me with a small smile. "Kind of makes you wonder, right?"

I laughed. "No. It does not make me wonder *at all*." I stepped aside and motioned toward the other man's retreating form. "But if you…"

"I don't." She waved me off. "Really…"

"I'd hate for you to feel like you're missing out on anything *big* because of me."

She looked up. "You mean you're not…?"

Whoa. "Oh yes I am," I told her. "In fact," I puffed up my chest. "People call me 'The *Biggest* One'…for lots of reasons," I teased, enjoying myself.

Until Leigh looked down and said, "The biggest jerk?"

Yeah. That'd been me. I let out a breath. "My granddad told me you mentioned you'd be at a big bonfire tonight. Based on you staying in Wainscott, I figured this would be the one. And yes, while I didn't exactly 'hunt you down,' I did come here specifically to see you…so I could apologize."

She crossed her arms over her chest again and stood there, looking at me.

"What?" I asked.

"I'm waiting." With the last remnants of the sun fading on

the horizon, I couldn't see her feet. If I could, I would bet she'd be tapping one of them. "For the apology."

Right. "I'm sorry," I said, meaning it.

Apparently Leigh didn't realize the significance of those two words coming from my mouth together, in that particular sequence, a phenomenon that didn't happen often, because she simply said, "For what? Calling me a prostitute in front of a patio full of people? Or insinuating I couldn't possibly be the kind of woman who would have an innocent meal with a nice old man without nefarious intent?"

If she hadn't been standing there looking so serious, the word 'nefarious' would have made me smile, but only because I'd bet my large but soon-to-be depleted bank account that the word 'nefarious' wasn't in the vocabulary of the beach bunny who'd sidled up to me earlier. I liked that it was a part of Leigh's vocabulary. Granddad was right. *She's a smart one.*

"I'm sorry for both — for everything that came out of my mouth." I stared down into her eyes. "For being the biggest jerk ever." She stood up to me, staring straight back, silent, as if waiting for more. I gave it to her. "I live a high-stress, fast-paced life that has gotten even more stressful since the health of both of my grandparents has started to decline."

She looked away. "You'll have to do better than that. In the past three months my dad had a heart attack and my grandpa had a stroke that left him incapacitated. I had to coordinate care for both of them, visit them in two different facilities, and pay their bills all while finishing up my senior year at Penn State. I still managed to graduate at the top of my class. *And*," she looked up at me. "I still managed to be nice to people."

Obviously she was a much better person than I was. But still, if this was a competition, I'd win for sure. "For the past year I've been basically supporting my grandparents in addition to myself. On Friday afternoon, a few hours before I showed up at the restaurant, forty employees at my company, myself included, got unceremoniously laid off. No warning. No severance. No 'thanks for working your ass off for the past two years.'"

She put her soft hand on my forearm. "Wow. That stinks."

Yup. Sure did. I covered her small hand with my larger one, my touch gentle, but keeping her there nonetheless.

"After cleaning out my cubicle I rushed to my apartment to dump the single, half-empty box that contained everything I had to show for two years of hard work and dedication, and rushed to catch the train out to the Hamptons, only to find my granddad and his car gone. He knows I don't like him driving in summer traffic."

"He told me that."

"By the time I got to the restaurant I was already on the verge of losing it."

"Then you saw me…"

"And I lost it. And I am really, very sorry it happened. If I could take it all back I would. But I can't."

"It's okay."

"So I'm forgiven?" Easy as that?

She thought about it, then did something I hadn't expected. Taking back her hand, she held it out to me. "We haven't been formally introduced. My name is Leigh."

No last name. No problem. "Nick," I said, shaking her

hand. "Nick Kenzy. It's a pleasure to meet you, Leigh." A total pleasure. More so tonight than the first time.

"Nice to meet you, too."

I could just make out her smile in the moonlight. I smiled back, realizing I'd smiled more in the past half hour than I had in months. "So we're good? I can report back to my granddad that I'm forgiven, and you don't think poorly of him because of me?"

"Yes. And please give him my regards."

"He had a great time with you. In fact, I can't get him to stop talking about you." Not that I minded.

She turned to look out at the ocean. "If only I had the same effect on guys my own age."

Did she hang around a bunch of limp-dick morons? The woman was kind and well-spoken, classy and gorgeous. "I'm sure you do."

She shook her head. "I'm too serious, too smart, too involved with my family."

"Those aren't bad things." In fact, they were qualities I very much respected.

She glanced over toward the party. "I should get back. My friends will wonder what happened to me."

After seeing how the blond kept an eye on Leigh, I was actually pretty surprised they'd given us this long to talk. With the thought of Leigh leaving, I realized I didn't want our time together to end. I liked her, and wanted to get to know her better. Hmmm. "I know I have no right to ask. That I am totally overstepping the bounds of our tenuous, dare I call it, friendship. But would you do me a favor?"

She looked up at me warily.

I held up both hands. "Nothing crazy. I was just wondering if you'd be willing to come by my granddad's place for dinner next week. I'm not a great cook, but I can barbecue a pretty good burger. Or steaks. Or I could probably do chicken or shrimp." Anything. Just say yes.

"I don't know." She took a step back.

I wasn't ready to give up. "Right. I get it. You don't know me. I mean, really know me, and here I am inviting you back to my place, which is really not much different than the Big One inviting you back to his, although my intentions are totally honorable. I swear." I put my hand over my heart for effect.

She didn't believe me.

"You see, since grandma died, granddad has let his house go. It's a mess, newspapers and magazines and food wrappers all over the place. The sink is overflowing with dishes. I offered to hire a cleaning lady once a week, but he refused, doesn't want some stranger in his house. Whenever I visit and try to clean we wind up getting into a huge fight." I hated fighting with him. "He says he'll do it. I know he won't do it. But if I were to go home tonight and tell him I invited you for dinner, he'd have to let me clean. Hell, he'd probably help because he'd want to make a good impression. So you'd really be doing me a big favor if you'd say yes."

There I was, bartering my granddad to get a date. But the reason behind my suggesting the barbecue was a valid one.

She took a little longer to think about it than I would have liked, so I added, "You can bring your friends."

That seemed to get her to relax a bit. Good.

She reached inside her string backpack. "Give me your number."

I did. Gladly. She programmed it into her phone. "Do you have a specific day in mind?" she asked.

"Nope. My schedule is completely open." It's not like I had a job to go to come Monday.

"Let me see what my friends and I have going on next week. Then I'll give you a call."

"Perfect." And she was. Absolutely perfect.

Chapter Five

Leigh

Five days later, I arrived at Murphy's house just before six o'clock. He lived in an older neighborhood about half an hour from the beach. Small houses on small lots, some better maintained than others. With summer traffic, the trip had taken me close to an hour.

Murphy's house was one of the better maintained ones, which surprised me, after what Nick had said about his granddad letting things go after his wife had died.

Murphy watched from the screened door as I exited my car. He had a big smile on his face, and I found myself very happy to see him again. "Come in." He opened the door, stepping to the side to make room for me.

"I brought dessert," I said, handing him the small bakery box and a container of cut up fruit I'd picked up in town.

"Hmmm," Murphy said. "What's in the box?" His eyes lit up in anticipation of my answer.

"You'll have to wait until after dinner to find out," I teased.

"As if he'd wait to peek inside," Nick said, joining us in the entryway, looking so handsome and relaxed in a pair of tan cargo shorts and a pale orange tank that looked great against his tanned skin, his dark hair mussed, like he'd finger-combed it after his shower. "Man's had a sweet tooth for as long as I've known him. Even though his doctor told him he needs to knock it off and show some restraint."

Murphy took the box without comment and walked away. I assumed to the kitchen, leaving Nick and me alone in awkward silence. I tried not to stare at the well-defined muscles on his arms. I'd never found a muscular man appealing before. Before? I swallowed, looking down at the dusting of hair on his equally muscled legs. Then, before I could stop myself, "Despite your busy schedule, you obviously make time for the gym," tumbled out of my mouth.

I felt my face heat.

He smiled.

Shaking my head, I told him, "I'm not good at this." In the classroom and in all matters of business, I could articulate with confidence. With my dad's friends and associates, I communicated with ease. I had no problems talking with senior citizens, and with my friends, meaningful, helpful and even funny words flowed effortlessly. But in social situations, outside of my comfort zone...? There was a reason I preferred to be home alone.

"You're very good at this," Nick said, completely serious.

I appreciated that, and started to relax, looking around the small family room, everything clean and neat. "Looks great."

"We've been working almost day and night since I told Murphy I'd invited you over, but we did it."

"Chocolate cake!" Murphy called out. "She brought us chocolate cake."

I couldn't help but smile at the excitement in his voice.

"It's for dessert," Nick called back. "Put it in the refrigerator." But he was smiling too, his affection for his grandfather evident. I liked that.

When Murphy walked back into the room, I told him, "You have a lovely home."

"My Lilly liked to keep a nice house," he said.

"Well, she'd be proud to see you keeping it up so nicely in her absence."

Murphy glanced over at Nick. "*Someone* finally put a much needed fresh coat of paint on the front porch.

"Only because *someone* finally *let* me put a much needed fresh coat of paint on the front porch."

I looked back and forth between them, unable to contain my smile. "You two are like an old married couple."

Murphy leaned in, cupped his hand at the side of his mouth, and, in a loud whisper, said, "My Lilly was much prettier than he is."

"I don't know," I said, looking Nick up and down. "He looks very pretty to me." What? I fought the urge to slap my hand over my mouth to keep anything else embarrassing from coming out. He wasn't pretty. He was handsome and confident and sexy. Enticing. And there I stood, looking him over…again.

What the heck was wrong with me?

Hormones.

No! Not hormones. Definitely not hormones. Simple sexual attraction. That was all.

"Luckily, I'm secure enough in my manhood to take that as a compliment," Nick said with a smile. "So thank you." He looked me up and down in return. "I think you're very pretty, too."

That made me happy. I'd worked very hard to look pretty tonight, trying on at least six outfits before Storme picked out this simple navy blue and white maxi dress with thick stripes, spaghetti straps, and a tie at the waist that gave me a nice shape – according to Storme.

"Come out on the deck," Nick said, guiding me in that direction with his hand at the small of my back. I loved it when men did that.

"I made fresh iced tea and lemonade," Murphy said.

"Or there's beer or wine," Nick added.

"You boys went all out," I noted. "Thank you." I looked toward Murphy. "A glass of lemonade would be perfect."

The deck was shaded by tall trees and overlooked a lovely backyard lined with flowers and a white wooden fence. What really caught my attention, though, was the patterned china plates set on the glass patio table.

Nick noticed me looking, and said, "I told granddad paper plates would be fine, but he insisted on going all out."

Murphy returned with two tall glasses of lemonade. "Lilly would have wanted me to set a nice table for our special guest."

So sweet. "Well, the table looks lovely, and I'm honored. Thank you."

Murphy shot a look at Nick that seemed to say, "See? I told you so."

"Would you grab me a beer?" Nick asked Murphy.

When he was gone, Nick whispered, "I still haven't told him I lost my job. He thinks I'm home on a two week vacation… Please don't mention it."

"Of course. And the house really does look great."

"Because of you," he said with appreciation.

"Because of *you*," I countered. "You did all the hard work."

Dinner was nice, the hamburgers delicious, the conversation smooth and enjoyable, and the atmosphere calm and friendly. All too soon Murphy glanced at his watch, said, "Time for Jeopardy," and got up from the table, leaving Nick and me alone.

"Yes," Nick said. "We live our lives according to the television schedule around here." He smiled so at ease. I envied that.

"Maybe I should…" I pushed back my chair, planning to clear my dishes.

"Sit," Nick said. "Relax. Let's enjoy this beautiful night."

Beautiful indeed, the air warm but with a refreshing breeze. "It's so peaceful here." It reminded me of the back porch at my dad's house.

"I love this area. I grew up in the next town over."

That surprised me. "Then how'd you wind up in New York City?"

He smiled. "I love the city, too." His smiled died. "When I didn't have money there were so many things I wanted to do but couldn't. When I finally had the money, I didn't have the time or energy. And now…" He looked into the backyard.

I put my hand over his. "You'll find something."

He turned back. "I know." He glanced down at our hands. "But how long will it take? Will I make enough to keep my apartment and keep granddad living here?"

I liked his concern for his grandfather. Despite my initial impression, Nick Kenzy was a good guy.

"Will I have to work the same insane schedule?" he went on. "While life passes me by, only to be unceremoniously fired, again, when my new company fails to meet projected earnings? Or when there's a downturn in the market? Or when the CEO wants a raise and there's not enough money in the budget to give him one?"

"I recently read about a CEO who took a cut in pay to give all of the employees in his company a raise." I tried to lighten the mood.

Nick let out an unhappy laugh. "Trust me, honey. A CEO willing to do that is the rarity, not the norm."

He looked tired and worn out. I started to stand again, wanting to give him time alone to rest.

He stopped me again, this time with a hand on my arm. "I'm sorry." He finished off his second bottle of beer. "Here you are fresh out of college, all wide-eyed and ready to take on the world. And here I sit, two years out of college, unemployed, cynical, beat up and spit out by Wall Street."

What could I possibly say that would make him feel better? Nothing came to mind, so I said nothing.

After a minute or two, Nick looked over at me and said, "You're not like the majority of women I know."

"That's a problem?" Of course it was.

"No." He shook his head. "Far from it, actually. I like that you're comfortable with silence, that you don't feel the need to fill it with idle chit chat and 'look on the bright' side bullshit."

"Not every situation has a bright side," I said, knowing that from experience.

"Very pragmatic of you."

"It's a character flaw."

He smiled. "No it's not." He stood. "Come with me." He walked behind my chair and eased it back as I stood. Such a gentleman. "I want to show you my grandmother's pride and joy."

"Beside you, you mean?"

He smiled again. "Yes, besides me."

I followed him down the deck stairs to the yard below. In the far corner were dozens of rose bushes in full bloom, vibrant pinks, yellows, peaches and reds. "They're…" lovely didn't do them justice, so I decided on, "…exquisite."

"Like you," he said.

I felt myself blush, only he didn't see it because he'd turned his back on me and was walking to a small red shed. A moment later he returned with some type of clipper, cut one of the peach roses and handed it to me.

When he went to cut another one, I reached for his hands. "Don't."

He clipped a second long stem, with a pink bud this time. "My grandmother would have wanted me to share her treasured roses with the person responsible for bringing happiness back to her husband's life." Then he handed me a perfect yellow bloom.

"Wow." I smiled. "You never say or do the wrong thing around women, do you?"

He turned to me all serious. "When we first met I called you a prostitute."

Yes, he had, but I was over that. "You did?" I brought the fragrant flowers up to my nose. "I'd forgotten all about that."

"Thank you." Then he stood there, watching me.

"What?" Did I have ketchup on my face? Something in my nose?

"I like you, Leigh."

Uh… "I like you, too, Nick." I really did.

"Would you go out to dinner with me? Just the two of us?"

The words, *Oh yes, I'd love to*, balanced on the tip of my tongue, ready to fly out of my mouth, only things were a little complicated for me right now. I couldn't, in good conscience, move forward without…

"Nick…" I hesitated, trying to figure out how much to tell him and where to start.

"You have a boyfriend."

"No."

"You—"

"Might be pregnant," came out of my mouth. Based on the shocked look on Nick's face, those were the absolute last words he'd expected to hear.

Chapter Six

Leigh

"It's a bit of a shocker for me, too," I told Nick as I studied the roses, avoiding eye contact, regretting my brutally honest words. Why couldn't I have simply said, "Yes," when he'd asked me if I had a boyfriend? Why couldn't I have come up with any explanation that didn't include the word 'pregnant?'

Because I really liked him, damn it, and if we were going to be spending time together, he deserved to know. Because I'd been feeling so alone and in need of someone to talk to, and Nick was so easy to talk to. Because maybe it wouldn't…maybe he…maybe we could…

"*Might* be pregnant?" he asked.

"Yes." I turned to face him. "Might be."

"I'm no expert, but isn't there a test you can take to find out for sure?"

I nodded. "But if I am, I'd rather not know just yet." I went on to tell him about Storme's wedding at the end of the summer, and how Kelsey, Storme and I had planned to have a fun summer to remember before we began our responsible adult lives – or I began life as a single parent.

"What about the guy?"

I couldn't bring myself to look at Nick, so I walked over to some pretty multi-colored pansies and spoke to them instead. "He's an old family friend. He's doing his residency in cardiology at a hospital near my hometown. I'd brought dad there with chest pain, again. His doctor admitted him for more testing. When visiting hours were over, dad had said good-bye to me like it might be the last time we were going to see each other, which devastated me because we're very close."

I walked over to some purple flowers I'd never seen before. "My friend saw me sitting in my car, crying. He took me out for a late dinner. Turned out he and his girlfriend were taking a break. I was heartsick; he was heartbroken. One thing led to another." I shrugged. "I'm not an impulsive person or a risk-taker." I bent down to pluck a weed. "That night, upset and stupid, I was both. Now there's a good chance I'm paying the price."

"What does the guy have to say about this possible pregnancy?"

I didn't answer, suddenly nauseous.

Nick walked to stand beside me. "Leigh?"

"He doesn't know." A thorn stuck me, so I brought my finger up to my mouth to suck off the blood. "He's busy with med school." I turned away. "And the girlfriend he'd been taking a break from? Well, apparently one almost night with me sent him running back to her. Now they're engaged."

"One *almost* night?"

Now for the humiliating truth, "We didn't…" finish. "He stopped…" before we'd really gotten started. "He felt guilty…" I swallowed, "because he was in love with someone else." I pushed some hair behind my ear. "And in an uncharacteristic demonstration of morning after stupidity, I didn't seek out emergency birth control, because I didn't think we'd done enough for me to need it." But it turned out we had.

"I don't know what to say. That sucks? I'm sorry he's engaged to another woman? "

"It's not like I'd want him to marry me instead of her. I don't. He doesn't love me, and I don't love him, and I'm perfectly capable of taking care of a child on my own." I walked a little farther down. "It's just that I can't decide if I should tell him now or wait until after he's married. I don't want to be responsible for ruining the happiness he's found with a really wonderful woman. I've met her. They're perfect for each other."

"You don't think he should have a say in what happens?"

I snapped my head in his direction. "A say in what happens? As in whether I keep the baby or not?"

"Whoa." Nick held up both hands. "All I'm saying is, if it were me, I'd want to know."

"To what end? I believe in a woman's right to choose, but abortion is not an option for me. That's the only decision that needs to be made right now, and I've made it."

"What do your friends have to say?"

I swallowed, reaching for another weed.

"So you haven't told them because you don't want to ruin their summer or Storme's wedding preparations," Nick said. "And you haven't told the future father—"

"*Possible* future father," I clarified.

Nick nodded in acknowledgement. "...because you don't want to disrupt his life. What about you?"

"Me? I'm eating healthy, taking a daily multivitamin and avoiding alcohol. For now that's all I need to do. Hopefully over the next few weeks my body will relax and I'll find out I'm not pregnant."

"And if you are?"

"If I am...then at least I had one amazing summer before the future I'd planned so carefully and worked so hard for completely falls apart." Up until then, those words had just been floating around in my head. Hearing them sent tears to my eyes. Hard as I tried, I couldn't stop them. Then, Lord help me, I sniffled.

Before I knew what was happening, strong arms turned me and wrapped around me and held me against a nice firm chest. "You're smart and competent. You'll find a way to make everything work out."

I nodded. "That's what I keep telling myself." I pulled away, wiping my eyes. "I'm sorry about that. It just feels so good to finally talk to someone about it. Although," I fidgeted with my flowers. "Sorry that someone turned out to be you."

"I'm not." He reached out and wiped a tear from my cheek. "I've gotta say. You are the sexiest possibly pregnant woman I've ever seen."

I laughed. I especially liked that he could make me laugh right then.

"So..." He lifted my chin so I had to look at him. "About that dinner."

I tried to turn my head, he wouldn't let me. "Now you see why it's probably not a great idea."

"I don't see that at all. If you're okay with going out on a date with an occasionally grumpy, out of work cynic, then I'm perfectly okay with going out on a date with a kind and considerate, very nice to look at, possibly pregnant woman. I think it'll be fun."

Maybe, but, "I don't know."

"Look. I'm here. You're here. I like you and you like me...at least, you said you did."

"I do."

"We've both got uncertain futures. So what? Let's take some time to let loose and play, to have a 'Summer of Fun.' I think we'd be good together, Leigh. What do you say?"

I wanted to say yes. I really, really wanted to say yes.

So I did. "Yes." Then I added, "But on one condition." I looked him straight in the eyes. "No asking me..." Hmmm. I wasn't used to discussing my period with men. "You know..."

His eyes lit with humor. "Deal." He held out his hand. "As long as you don't ask me how the job search is going."

"Deal." I shook his hand, looking forward to the next few weeks.

The next day I sat on a plump, pink chair in the viewing area of an upscale bridal boutique, a glass of champagne in my hand, while a saleswoman assisted Storme in the dressing room.

"What do you think about Storme marrying Phillip?" I asked Kelsey, who sat to my left. "Something feels off to me." I set my glass down, knowing one sip and I wouldn't be able to stop myself from drinking the rest. I shifted in my seat to face my friend. "Her face doesn't light up when she talks about him." I reached into my purse for a breath mint. "It's almost like she's resigned to marrying him but not excited about it. In my opinion, she spends more time talking about merging vineyards and wedding plans than she does talking about the groom."

"I noticed that, too."

"And she's so young."

"Maybe he's an animal between the sheets," Kelsey said.

We looked at each other and both broke out laughing. "Nah," she said. "It's got to be something else."

Although Phillip was handsome and paid a lot of attention to his grooming and clothing, there was nothing sexy about him, at least not in my opinion. Not like Nick, anyway. He was too polite, too accommodating, too…effeminate, for lack of a better word. But he was also sweet and kind, and he treated Storme like a princess.

"Ladies," the saleswoman said. "Are you ready?"

Kelsey and I turned in her direction as Storme exited the dressing room and stepped up onto the round platform surrounded on three sides by floor to ceiling mirrors.

Oh, my God. I reached for a tissue.

After looking at herself, she turned to face us, and I lost my ability to speak. My best friend in the world was getting married, and she looked absolutely amazing. Tears filled my eyes.

"You look gorgeous, Storme," Kelsey said, keeping it together much better than I was. "Prettier than any *Modern Bride* magazine cover."

"Stunning," I added. "Elegant."

"Do you really like it?" Storme looked unsure, which struck me as odd. She knew fashion better than anyone, knew what looked good on her and virtually every other body type. She could have been a designer, if not for her parents pulling her back into the family business. Yet she was unsure about her own wedding dress?

"I love it," I said.

"So do I," Kelsey agreed.

The gown had a sweetheart neckline and tight-fitting bodice that showcased Storme's figure. It sparkled when she moved, thousands of crystals catching the light.

"What about the veil?" Storme asked, turning slightly. "I went with long and plain. I could change to short or one with more detail." She looked toward the saleswoman, who nodded.

"I think the one you're wearing is perfect," I said.

"I agree," Kelsey said. "Plain is good. You want people looking at your dress, not your veil."

Storme bunched up the tulle skirt in her hands and stuck out a foot to show us her shoes. "I had these specially made to match."

A white satin, open-toed beauty, with a slender four-inch heel and beading that matched her bodice.

"Only you," Kelsey said. "They look like they cost a fortune."

"They did." Storme turned back to the mirrors. "But a girl only gets married once, right?" She smiled, but to me it looked forced. "And she should look like a princess on that day, don't you think?"

"She should look a lot happier than you're looking right now," I said. "What's going on, Storme?"

Kelsey poured a glass of champagne, stood, and handed it to Storme. "You look like you need this."

Storme drank the entire glass and handed it back empty.

Kelsey re-filled it.

"I..." Storme glanced at the saleswoman.

Kelsey jumped out of her chair like it was on fire. "Not now, please. We have a crisis."

Following her lead, I jumped to my feet, too. "Yes, no interruptions, please," I told the saleswoman. "And more champagne."

The woman's worried eyes dropped to Storme's dress, but she nodded. "Would you like to slip out of your dress first?" she asked.

"She's fine," Kelsey answered. Then, to Storme, she said, "Come on, princess." She held out her hand. Storme took it and stepped off the platform.

I helped Storme maneuver in her gown. "Sit here." I directed her to the chair I'd been sitting in and pulled up another one to sit facing her.

Kelsey re-filled Storme's glass. She drank that one down, too.

Not good.

"What's going on?" Kelsey asked.

"Talk to us," I said. "We're your friends. You can tell us anything."

"Are you holding out on us, Storme?" Kelsey asked.

Storme sniffed, then took a sip of champagne.

I lifted my glass and took a small sip, too.

After sharing something major lacking in her and Phillip's relationship, Storme looked down at her lap, and said, "I'm not even married yet, and I'm thinking about having an affair."

Oh. My. God.

Chapter Seven

Nick

After our barbecue, Leigh had stuff planned with her friends, including a bridal fitting. We'd spoken on the phone one night into the early morning hours, about poker, among other things, neither one of us wanting to end the call. I smiled, trying to picture sweet Leigh taking on a bunch of hardcore gamblers at a Texas Hold'em tournament in Atlantic City. That's where her grandfather had taken her to celebrate her twenty-first birthday. She'd finished in the top twenty out of over two hundred entrants, winning a one thousand dollar prize.

The more I learned about her, the more I wanted to know.

The next day she'd headed home to visit her dad and grandfather, which gave me time to finally do the employment stuff I'd neglected while helping granddad clean up his house and yard. Resumé updated and e-mailed to five head hunters, I'd considered browsing some help wanted sites...but only for a few seconds. It was a beautiful summer day, and granddad had taken the bus to the senior center.

So, I headed for the beach.

Thankfully, Murphy had thought to get a beach parking pass – the reason I was driving his very late model, maroon Pontiac instead of my relatively new silver Mercedes, which I kept parked in his garage. Not much need for a car in the city.

After finding a spot of sand close to the water, I dropped my towel, chair and keys, then stripped off my shirt and set out for a nice long swim, like the good old days. The water looked relatively calm, but calm could be deceiving. It hid strong currents, which I fought through, to remain on course. By the time I finished, my arms and legs felt like lead weights. I set up my chair, plopped into it and closed my eyes, welcoming the heat on my cool, wet skin, letting the sun bake the color of life – as Jake had called it – back into me.

As my body relaxed, my heart rate and breathing slowed. A female giggle caught my attention. It sounded close. Me, being a guy and all, I opened my eyes, using my hand as a visor to shield the sun. Three young women, all nice looking from the back, early twenties by my estimation, stood a few feet away, letting the waves wash over their ankles.

In the not too distant past I would have come up with a reason to strike up a conversation, or created an opportunity to interact with them. But today, thoughts of Leigh filled my mind, like how fantastic she'd look in one of those skimpy string bikinis and how much I looked forward to seeing her in one.

It caught me off guard, because she might be pregnant… with another man's baby. I should have taken the chance she'd offered to rescind my dinner invitation and used my time in the Hamptons to search out an uncomplicated woman looking for a fun, sex-filled summer fling.

Yet I hadn't. I felt drawn to Leigh and wanted to be there for her. If anyone could give her a summer of fun, I could. At the expense of a fun summer for myself?

No, I didn't think so. I enjoyed her company, liked talking to her and looking at her and making her blush. And I was really looking forward to spending more time with her, which made me wonder when she'd be back? I pulled my phone out of my bag, grabbing my water bottle at the same time. Taking a few chugs, I checked the time and decided to give her a call.

She answered on the third ring. "Hello?"

"It's Nick. How's your visit going?"

"Dad's doing well. My grandfather is the same. I'm on my way back to Storme's house."

The news gave me a little buzz of happy anticipation. "On your way back as in driving in the car right now? Are you okay to talk?"

"I'm hands free. You're coming at me through my speakers in surround sound."

I smiled. "How'd your bridal fitting go?"

She didn't answer right away. Uh oh. "Leigh?"

"Yes. I'm here. The bridal fitting was…enlightening."

Not a word I'd expected, but okay. "Care to elaborate?"

"Not really, except to say after what I learned, I have some doubts as to whether Storme's wedding will be taking place as scheduled."

"Oh boy."

"Tonight the three of us are having dinner together. Storme really needs Kelsey and me right now."

My little buzz of happy anticipation faded. "Oh."

"But I was thinking, if you want to hang out, and absolutely no pressure if you don't, but if you do, maybe you could stop by the house later on for a walk on the beach? We could discuss plans for our 'Summer of Fun.'

I liked the sound of that...but waited a few seconds to respond so I didn't sound overly eager. "That'd be great."

"I'll text you the address. Say around nine?"

"Perfect." Sure it'd be dark, so I'd have to wait a little longer to see her in a bathing suit. But that was okay, because maybe, just maybe, it felt a little odd to be lusting after a possibly pregnant woman. "Is it weird that I hardly know you, yet I can't stop thinking about you, and I'm really looking forward to seeing you tonight?" And that I felt perfectly comfortable telling her that?

"I hope not, because I can't stop thinking about you either, and I'm really looking forward to seeing you tonight, too."

Yes!

"In all the time I've been spending alone in this car," Leigh said. "I've come to the conclusion it's probably because I'd rather think about you than...other things. And keeping secrets is exhausting. But since you know mine and I know yours, we don't have to pretend everything's okay or be on guard around each other. We can just be ourselves, and there's something very appealing about that."

Appealing indeed. "You mean it's not because I'm handsome

and sexy, and you want to jump my bones?" I teased.

"That's not the main reason, no," she said.

Shucks.

"But it is an added bonus."

I laughed. God, I liked her.

"Okay. Lots of traffic. I need to concentrate."

"Drive carefully. See you tonight."

"Bye."

After putting away my phone, I went back to sunbathing, my mind on Leigh and all the fun things I wanted to do with her this summer...clothes on and clothes off.

Later that night I knocked on the door of a truly spectacular Wainscott mansion, feeling under-dressed in my shorts, flip flops and old college sweatshirt.

Leigh opened the door with a smile that warmed my insides. "Hi." She handed me a glass of white wine. "Quick," she whispered. "Drink this."

Anything for a friend. "Damn." I looked at the empty glass. "That was good."

"Storme's family owns a vineyard." Leigh stared at my lips, then lifted her thumb to the corner of my mouth. "You have a little…" She touched me, her skin so soft, her scent enticing. It was all I could do not to turn my head the tiniest bit and suck her finger into my mouth. As if she could read my dirty mind, she retracted her arm with a jerk. "Sorry. I shouldn't have…"

I reached for her hand and dropped a kiss on her knuckles. "You can touch me," I lifted my eyes to hers, "anytime you want.

Anywhere you want. 'Summer of Fun,' remember?"

She blushed.

I really liked that blush.

"Please." She stepped back. "Come in."

I followed her to a large, nicely furnished living room where her two friends sat on a large sofa, each holding a glass of wine. Leigh set her empty one on the coffee table.

"Nick, meet my friends. Storme," she motioned to the brunette. "And Kelsey." The blond smiled and gave me a wave.

I shook each woman's hand. "Let me guess," I said. "Little red Mercedes convertible." I pointed to the stylish Storme. "And sweet Shelby Mustang." I pointed to the down-to-earth Kelsey. "What year?"

"Sixty-eight," Kelsey said, with a nod of approval.

"Does she ride as good as she looks?"

"Better." She smiled.

Storme stood. "Would you like a glass of wine, Nick?"

"No, thank you." Just had one. "I'm good." I glanced at Leigh. She wouldn't look at me.

Storme sat back down, studying me as if trying to determine if I was good enough for Leigh. I probably wasn't, but that didn't stop me from wanting her. "What do you do for a living, Nick?"

"He's an analyst on Wall Street," Leigh answered for me.

"Just like your—" Kelsey started.

"Time to go," Leigh interrupted, grabbing my hand and pulling me toward a pair of sliding doors at the back of the room. "We'll be walking on the beach."

"Should we wait up?" Storme called from behind us, teasing.

I looked over my shoulder, "No," and gave them a smile and a wave. "Nice meeting you both."

The doors opened to an equally spectacular deck with an outdoor kitchen barbecue station to the right and a large pool to the left. A set of stairs led to a lower deck with a whirlpool tub that'd seat at least eight, and there was a stone fire pit to the right. Although I couldn't see it in the dark, I heard the ocean waves close by.

Growing up, a house like this had been my dream, even only to rent one for the summer. But after two years spent working toward that dream, after losing myself in eighty hour work weeks, missing out on time with my family and friends, and almost killing myself to impress unappreciative bosses, I had to wonder if it was worth it?

Since meeting Leigh, I found myself concentrating on the here and now rather than the future, on enjoying each day and night to the fullest. I followed her down another flight of stairs that led to the beach, appreciating the movement of her shapely ass beneath her cotton dress shorts, and those long, bare legs...

When we reached the sand, she removed her tan boat shoes and set them neatly to the side of the bottom step. I kicked off my flip flops, leaving them where they landed. A gust of wind blew sand at us. Leigh turned her head away. I debated suggesting she run back inside for a jacket or sweatshirt, but she looked so sweet and proper in her soft white cardigan. And I'd be happy to warm her up if she needed warming.

The wind died down, and we walked toward the waves, guided by the moonlight.

"Look." Leigh pointed. "Fireworks."

Off in the distance. "Yeah, people shoot them off on the beach all the time." Even though they weren't supposed to.

"I love fireworks," she said, stopping to watch them.

"If you're still here, they do a pretty nice fireworks show on Main Beach the Saturday of Labor Day Weekend."

She looked off toward the water. "I'm leaving right after Storme's wedding. I won't be here," she said, with a hint of sadness in her voice.

I made a mental note to check around for any other local fireworks shows before that.

We reached the water and Leigh walked in up to her ankles. I joined her, taking in the beautiful night, the soothing ebb and flow of the water.

"Oh!" Leigh jumped back, grabbing onto me. "Something touched my foot." She looked down, so I did, too, even though we could barely see our feet.

"Fish," I laughed, holding her, enjoying the feel of her.

She stepped away. "Sorry, I—"

"Don't be." I turned. "Come on." I held out my hand. "Let's walk."

She hesitated. For a few seconds, I thought she might leave me hanging, but she didn't, sliding her hand into mine as if she'd done it dozens of times before. It fit perfectly, felt like it belonged there.

We walked in silence, me closer to the water, the packed wet sand giving under my feet, each of us lost in our own thoughts. I couldn't remember the last time I'd looked forward to seeing a woman as much as I'd looked forward to seeing Leigh tonight. I couldn't remember ever feeling this comfortable with a woman...or this content. I wanted to kiss her, to take her in my arms, hold her tight against my body and show her how much I wanted her.

"What are you thinking about?" she asked as we walked.

I told her the truth. "You."

She stopped and turned to me, even more beautiful in the moonlight, her hair blowing wild. "What about me?"

I let go of her hand, to free up both of mine which I set on her hips. "How comfortable I feel with you in such a short time. How attracted I am to you. How much I want to kiss you." No moment had ever felt so right.

"Then kiss me," she said, stepping closer, tilting her lips up to mine.

Chapter Eight

Leigh

He moved his hands from my hips to cup my cheeks. Then he pressed his lips to mine so carefully and tenderly, his touch gentle. I didn't know if it was the moonlit night, or the cool ocean breeze, or the sound of the waves that made the moment feel so romantic or if it was the man himself that affected me, that ignited something deep inside of me and made me want…more.

Needing something to do with my hands, I slid them up under the back of his sweatshirt, and flattened them on his soft, warm skin.

He moaned, deepening the kiss, moving one of his hands to the back of my head and the other to my butt, where he tugged my hips in close, letting me feel his arousal.

I rubbed against it shamelessly. Never had a man affected

me this way. Well, once a man had come close, but my need had been more emotional than physical and the possible…probable consequences had me turning away. "You tempt me to do bad things."

He pulled me closer. "What kind of things?"

"Sex on the beach kind of things." Meaningless sexual summer fling kind of things. Things a woman in my possible… condition shouldn't be considering.

He smiled. "You tempt me, too."

"But I can't…"

He lifted his head and let out a frustrated breath. "God, Leigh. No buts. 'Summer of Fun,' remember? Two weeks down, only six to go."

"I don't want you to think that because I may be…" I was starting to despise the word pregnant.

"Knocked up?"

That would do. "Yes, knocked up. I don't want you to think I'm easy or that I sleep around, because I don't."

"Honey, the last thing I want to do with you is sleep." Hair blew across my face, and he carefully pushed it aside. "I want to do wide awake things. Fun things." He pulled me close and nuzzled up to my ear. "Arousing things." He let out a hot, moist breath that shot tingles straight into my jaw.

"And naked things, no doubt."

He leaned back to look at me, smiling. "Well, now that you brought it up…" he teased.

"Mommy, look," a young voice said. "Ewww. They're kissing."

No, we weren't, but still. I tried to jump away.

As if anticipating I might, Nick held me tight. "We're being watched," he whispered, not concerned at all.

"I'm really not into that," I whispered back, trying to push out of his arms.

He laughed, still not letting me go.

"Honestly," a woman huffed. "You'd think *people* would be more considerate of the fact there are children on the beach." I imagined her covering her child's eyes and dragging him or her away from our indecent public display.

"It's late," I whispered. "Shouldn't her child be in bed instead of out on the beach?"

"Children ruin everything," Nick said in my ear. No sooner were the words out of his mouth than he stiffened. "I'm sorry. I didn't mean—"

"It's okay." I twisted, and this time he let me go. "I'm guessing a lot of guys feel that way about kids." Suddenly cold, I crossed my arms over my chest. "I might find myself saying the exact same thing in a few months."

"Leigh. I didn't mean—"

I couldn't look at him. Instead, I stared out at the ocean. "I know." Even so, his words made my chest ache.

"Leigh." He took me by the shoulders and turned me to face him. "Don't do this. Don't think about what may or may not happen after the summer. Let's enjoy the time we have together, right now. Tonight."

I wanted to, I really did. But tears leaked into my eyes. Maybe they glistened in the moonlight, because Nick saw them and looked stricken. "I am such an ass." He drew me into a hug. "I'm sorry."

Unable to speak, I nodded, more tears coming. His arms felt good, so strong and safe. I would have liked nothing more than to remain wrapped in his protective embrace forever, but I couldn't. "I'm sorry, too." I stepped back, wiping my eyes. "I'm not usually emotional." Yet, in the short time of our acquaintance, I'd already broken down into tears in front of Nick twice. Not a good sign.

"It's okay," he said. "You're under a lot of stress."

I hoped stress was the only reason.

"Come on." He held out his hand. "Let's keep walking."

I looked around, wondering where that awful woman had gone.

"I think she went that way." Nick pointed, reading my mind.

"Then we should go this way." I took a step in the opposite direction, which happened to be the way back to Storme's house.

That's the way we went, my hand in his, both of us quiet, until Nick said, "There are lots of fun things we can do around here with our clothes on, you know."

I smiled. "Like what?"

"Parasailing, stand up paddle boarding, wave runners. We can go hiking or biking or on a picnic."

"Or we could sit around Storme's pool and eat hot dogs. Or lie on the beach under an umbrella and read books."

"Since either one of those activities would give me a chance to see you in a bikini, yes to both."

"A bikini? You want to see me in a bikini?" How flattering.

"Yes, I do. Please tell me you brought one."

I'd brought three. "I guess you'll have to come over tomorrow afternoon to find out."

"It's a date."

We reached the portion of beach directly behind Storme's house way too soon. Rather than turning toward the stairs, Nick turned to face the ocean, positioning me to stand in front of him, so my back rested against his front, before clasping his hands at my waist. "It's a beautiful night."

Yes, it was, made even more beautiful because of the man standing behind me. I rested my head against his cheek. A wave rolled in. When the water receded, my feet sunk into the soft, wet sand.

"If you had one wish," he said. "One wish guaranteed to come true, and you could wish for anything, what would it be?"

So many things came to mind, starting with the greater good: World peace. An end to hunger, oppression, poverty or disease. Then to more personal matters: A negative pregnancy test result, but that would be selfish. Maybe an improvement in Grandpa's health or an end to Dad's heart condition.

"I can almost hear your mind at work trying to decide," Nick said.

"There are so many possibilities. I can't choose just one."

"But you only have one wish," he said, as if he actually had the ability to grant it. If only…

"I'll have to give it more thought." I gathered up some of my hair in my fist to keep it from blowing in his face. "What about you?" I asked. "What would you do with your one wish?"

He didn't hesitate. "Make love to you."

What? "You'd waste your one wish on having sex with me?"

"It wouldn't be a waste." He kissed my head. "And it wouldn't be just sex."

Not knowing what to say, I stood there in silence, until Nick said, “Do you want to know why?”

I nodded.

“You’re the total package, Leigh. Looks and brains, kindness and compassion. You’re something special, and I feel a real connection to you. Under different circumstances I’d have no problem taking it slow and seeing where things might lead. But who knows what’s going to happen at the end of the summer? What if right now is all we have? I want to make the most of every minute of our time together. I want to know everything there is to know about you.”

He turned me to face him and said, “So I’d selfishly use my one wish to make love to you, sooner rather than later.” He stared into my eyes, the intensity of his gaze warming me. “It already feels like the six weeks we have left isn’t going to be enough.”

The next day I sat at a table on the deck, under the umbrella, pretending to read on my Kindle, waiting for Nick. *It already feels like the six weeks we have left isn’t going to be enough.* My heart squeezed. I could really fall for that man…if circumstances were different.

“You’re awful quiet.” Storme sat down beside me, dressed for town.

“Just thinking.”

Kelsey sat down on the other side of me, wearing a bikini with a loose fitting tank. “You’ve been doing a lot of that lately.”

I had a lot to think about. “I invited Nick over today.” I

looked at Storme. "I hope that's okay."

"Of course it is. My house is your house."

I smiled, remembering when I'd first met Storme, three freshman squished into a dorm room meant for two. *What's mine is yours*, she'd said on that first day. "Thank you."

She leaned forward until she made eye contact with me. "You sure you're okay?"

I nodded, glancing away quickly, unable to look at her for fear she'd be able to see that I was not okay at all.

Thank goodness Nick chose that moment to walk up the back steps to the deck. "Good afternoon, ladies," he said with a big smile. Then he held up a grocery bag. "I brought dinner. That is, if you like hot dogs. If you don't," he held up a grocery bag in his other hand, "I brought snacks."

"I love both," Kelsey said. "But I'm not sure I'm going to be here for dinner." She glanced at her watch and stood. "Depends on how my afternoon at the beach turns out."

"Going to look for Sean?" Storme teased.

Sean Dempsey, AKA the Hampton Hottie, who just happened to be the lifeguard Kelsey had met the day she'd arrived in the Hamptons.

"Won't need to look hard," Kelsey said. "I know exactly where he's going to be." And with that, she left.

Storme stood. "I'm off, too. My wedding favors are in."

"Oh. Why didn't you say anything?" I asked. "I would have come with you." Isn't that something a maid of honor should do, go with the bride to check out her wedding favors?

"I know you would have," Storme said. "But then you'd have seen the very special gifts I ordered for you and Kelsey.

I couldn't have that, now, could I?" On her way back into the house, she looked over her shoulder. "You have the house all to yourselves. I'll probably grab a bite in town, so I won't be home for *hours*."

I felt my face heat. "Could you be more obvious?"

"Obvious?" Nick asked. "Obvious about what?"

Storme laughed, and then she was gone.

Leaving Nick and me alone. "So..."

"I should probably put some of this stuff in the refrigerator."

"Right. Sorry. Why didn't I think of that?" And why was I suddenly so nervous?

"Hey." I felt his hand on my shoulder. "Come here."

I turned, and he kissed me; a slow, sweet, caring kiss. "Relax."

I smiled, feeling a little shy. "Thanks, I needed that."

He smiled, too. "Any time."

After we'd put away the groceries, we went back outside.

"That's the pool cover-up you wore to the bonfire," Nick said approvingly.

"Storme made one for each of us." Beautifully styled to fall off one shoulder and show lots of leg, in a bold print I never would have purchased for myself, but that I'd grown to love.

"I like it," he said. "Now take it off."

"What?" I laughed. "You first."

He looked down at his lime green tank and baggy gray shorts. "Me first what?"

"I want to see you in your bathing suit first."

He pulled the tank over his head and held out his arms. "This is me in my bathing suit."

Man, he had a sexy chest, firm abs and muscled arms. But, "You're kidding, right?" I crossed my arms. "You want to see me in my little bikini, all of my goods on display. The least you could have done is worn a Speedo so I could see all of *your* goods on display."

I was teasing, of course.

But Nick got this serious look on his face, and he walked toward me, slowly, not stopping until I could smell his coconut-scented skin.

I swallowed.

"You want to see my goods?" He moved his hands to the front of his waistband. "Here? Or would you rather go inside?"

This had to stop. I hated feeling off balance around him, so I dug deep and found some self-confidence that had been lollygagging around of late. "Sorry." I looked him straight in the eyes. "I need a little more foreplay than 'you show me yours and I'll show you mine.'"

He laughed.

Whew.

Then he reached into his bag, pulled out a tube of suntan lotion, and held it up. "How about we try some hands-on activities?"

I walked over to him. "How about we let it happen when it happens and stop trying to force it?" I held out my hand. "But I'll be happy rub you with lotion if you'd like me to." Lord help me, that didn't come out the way I'd intended.

Nick hesitated, as if trying to decide how to proceed. "I'd like you to." He smiled a plain old, regular handsome smile. No innuendo, no lascivious intent.

I appreciated that. "Thank you for your restraint."

"It wasn't easy."

"I'm proud of you."

His smile grew. "I'm proud of me, too."

'You show me yours and I'll show you mine' may not have worked as foreplay for me, but rubbing lotion on Nick's bare back sure did. He stood before me as my moistened hands caressed him, his muscles defined, his shoulders rounded, his skin warm and smooth and tan. I rubbed up to his neck, down to his low back, up his sides, an activity I'd have been happy to perform all day. All too soon he said, "I think I'm done."

Well, *I* didn't think so, mostly because *I* didn't feel done. But okay. I forced myself to stop.

He spun around to face me, taking the lotion from my hand. "Now it's your turn." He seemed rather eager to get started.

The moment of truth had arrived. I put my hands on the hem of my pool cover-up, inhaled a fortifying breath, and lifted it over my head, tossing it onto a lounge chair.

At first I couldn't look at Nick. Well, I could have, but I didn't want to. Instead, I busied myself looking everywhere but. Then the silence got to me. So I dared a peek. He stood there, staring at me with an odd look on his face.

I glanced down. Boobs were covered, bottoms in place. "What's wrong?" I asked, feeling on display and uncomfortable because of it.

"You're…"

His eyes dropped to my lower abdomen. Feeling self-conscious, my hands went down there to hide it from view. I shouldn't have eaten those potato chips last night. This morning

I'd woken up bloated and gross, and this was a mistake. I grabbed for my cover-up.

"Don't." Nick got there first.

"Hasn't anyone told you it's impolite to stare?" I tried to yank my clothing out from under his hand.

He held on tight. "I'm sorry. It's just…you're stunning," he said, looking down the length of my legs.

Okay. He could keep the cover-up. "Thank you. But—"

Before I could finish, he said, "I think we both need to cool off." And he pushed me into the pool!

Chapter NINE

Nick

We had to cool off? More like *I* had to cool off. I threw myself into the pool after Leigh, hitting the cold water, welcoming the shock of it.

What the hell was wrong with me? I swam up to the surface. She'd asked me to tone it down, and I'd had every intention of doing just that. But then I'd felt her soft hands on my heated skin and saw her exquisite, almost nude body, those full breasts, just the way I like them, that thin waist and curvy thighs. Man oh man. My cock had developed a mind of its own and refused to abide to my 'tone it down' plan.

A few more seconds and Leigh would have gotten a very real, very large indication of my attraction. No words necessary.

"What the heck?" she said, popping up to tread water a few feet in front of me, the floppy straw hat she'd been wearing floating beside her.

I braced for the harsh words and anger sure to follow my impulsive, idiotic move. *You ruined my hair...my makeup...my hat.* I could have jumped in by myself, but nooo. I had to push Leigh in ahead of me. Idiot.

"I'll buy you a new hat," I said stupidly.

"That hat is an Octavio Florio Delgado original. It cost five thousand dollars."

"Five thousand dollars?" I plucked it out of the water and swam it over to the deck. "Are you kidding me?"

"Yes." A huge splash of water hit me in the back of the head. What the...? I turned to Leigh and wham! In came another one. I wiped my eyes and opened them to see her...smiling.

"You're going to pay for that," she said, splashing me again.

"Oh I am, am I?" Now I was smiling too.

"Yes." Splash. "You are."

I made a move toward her, and she dove under the water. The battle was on.

Something pulled at the bottom of my bathing suit. Not something, some-*one*. And I knew exactly who. I had half a mind to let her yank it clean off. Only right then I felt more like playing. So I dove under the water too...at the same time she came up for air.

A simple tug was all it took to untie her tiny top.

I resurfaced to hear her laughing. "You did not just do that." Treading water, she had her hand holding her bikini in place.

"I most certainly did." I smiled, enjoying myself immensely. When was the last time I'd played around in a pool? So long ago I couldn't remember. "What are you going to do about it?"

She quickly re-tied her top and swam toward me with a

determined look on her face. A few seconds later she had me in a headlock, her bikini-covered boob smushed into my eye, and she was trying to dunk me. Really?

No one, and I mean no one, bested me in a pool wrestling match…ever.

I had to admit, she was a wily thing, wrapping her legs around me, tightly, and holding on to the point I couldn't shake her loose. Ouch! My nipple. She fought dirty. "No pinching."

"No promises," was all she said in between her laughing.

So I dunked us both. While we were down there, I untied her bikini top, again, along with one of her bottom strings, too. What the hell. She'd started it.

Ouch! She pinched me again. Then she swam away.

I followed, with my eyes open, watching her underwater.

Down at the shallow end she stood, only her head above the water, one hand covering her top, the other holding her bottom together.

I resurfaced a distance away, giving her some space.

"Time out," she said.

That made me laugh. "Time out? What are we? Twelve?" It kind of felt like we were, and I kind of liked it.

She smiled. "I need a minute to get my bikini back under control."

Even though I preferred it the way it was, being the gentleman I am, I offered my assistance. "You need some help with that?"

She glared at me, but it was a playful glare. "No. I've got it." She turned her back to me and opted to fix her bottoms first. I used the opportunity of her distraction to very quietly and carefully swim closer.

Apparently not quietly or carefully enough because she caught me. "Stop."

I didn't. "Let me help you." I moved in behind her. "We want to make sure it's tied good and tight so that doesn't happen again." I took a string in each hand, holding them beneath her shoulder blades.

She glanced over her shoulder at me. "Yes. We do."

I'd gone over there intending to help. Really. But standing so close to her, something in my brain short-circuited. That's the only explanation I could come up with to explain why my hands were suddenly touching her, pulling her close, skin to skin.

Maybe something had short-circuited in her brain, too, because she let me, even going so far as to rest her head back on my shoulder.

I took it slow, not wanting to spook her, when going slow was the last thing I wanted. I smoothed my hands down her sides, over the indentation of her waist, to her hips.

"Don't." She stopped me at the ties to her bottom.

"I won't." Not yet.

My hands took a different route back, over her stomach. I felt her tighten her abs and smiled. "You're perfect."

"Far from it."

Close enough for me.

I reached her ribs and kept on going…beneath her bikini top, to the undersides of her breasts, round and full. I closed my eyes so nothing would distract me from the pure joy of feeling her for the very first time. I slid my hands forward, just a bit, and pinched each nipple, much gentler than she'd pinched mine a few minutes ago.

She let out a breath. "That feels nice."

Yes, it did. I pinched them again, a little harder.

She moaned and ground her butt back into me, and the tenuous hold I'd had on my self-control threatened to snap. I held it together…barely, sending one hand lower, between her legs. I stayed on the outside of her bathing suit, but moved my hand with purpose, touching her the way women liked to be touched down there.

"That feels so good." As she moved against my hand, her butt rubbed along my erection.

If she kept it up, we'd both come without me ever getting inside of her.

Ladies first.

When she rocked her hips back, I positioned my hand to skillfully slip beneath her bikini bottom on the upswing. It worked like a charm. I'd expected her to stiffen or stop me. She did neither.

"Okay?" I asked, my fingers moving through her short hair, dipping between her moist lips, along her wet heat, until I reached her opening.

"Yes," she said, breathless.

I slid inside.

"More," she whispered.

I added another finger, plunging deep. She squeezed them tight.

"I want you," I whispered in her ear. So fucking bad my cock ached. I swirled my hand, spreading her juices, then I pushed back in, with three fingers that time.

"I want you, too," she said, surprising me when she turned

around, threw her arms around my neck and her legs around my waist. She kissed me, honest to God, like I'd never been kissed before…with such passion…such desire.

"Hold on tight."

She did.

I carried her out of the water and over to an inflatable pool lounger lying in the corner of the massive deck. Bushes blocked its view from the neighbors. Three recliner chairs made it difficult to see from the pool. Yet somehow I'd spotted it earlier. Lucky me.

To protect her delicate skin, I grabbed a towel and threw it down to cover the plastic. Then I set her on her back.

"You'll need a—" She moved the towel around.

"I know." I reached into my pocket for the condom I'd stored there this morning. Just in case.

She undid the tie at her neck and flung the top away, her breasts an absolute vision of loveliness. "Even though I might—"

"I know." I knelt down, holding up the condom.

"Oh." She slid out of her bottoms, her hair even redder down there. "Good." She looked up at me. "Well, come on then."

I smiled, my hands going to the drawstring of my shorts. "In a hurry, are we?"

"If you'd rather not…"

She tried to roll off the float, but I tackled her. "Where do you think you're going?"

"I changed my mind."

I slid down and licked her nipple. "Give me a minute to change it back." I sucked hard, while shifting to the side so I could slide two fingers deep inside of her. Still so wet, she hadn't changed her mind at all.

She bent one knee and dropped it to the side, rocking her hips into my touch.

On the end of a moan, she said, "That feels good."

Unable to wait a second longer, I lifted to my knees.

Leigh went up on her elbows to watch as I lowered my shorts, not doing a thing to hide her blatant perusal of my package. "You like?" I ripped open the condom wrapper.

She nodded. "Very much."

I swelled even more. Condom on, I settled myself on top of her, naked skin to naked skin. "God, you feel amazing."

She opened her legs even wider.

Even better.

Cock in hand, I rubbed the tip up and down along her slit, dipping inside, just a bit, before retracing my path.

Leigh thrust her hips in invitation.

I stayed my course, over and over, waiting…

"Please," she said, her fingernails digging into my ass.

I gave her what we both wanted, driving deep, again and again. She met each thrust with one of her own. Fuck. Me. She felt so wet, so hot, so unbelievably good, my balls started to tingle. Too soon.

I wasn't going to last.

Shifting up, I slowed things down, angling my hips, making sure to hit her clit every time I moved.

"Ooohhh." She moaned. "I like that."

Good. I did, too.

She moaned again, lifting her knees, arms and legs holding me tight. "So good." She pumped her hips. "Don't stop."

A category five hurricane couldn't stop me. I was too far

gone, pounding into her, my moans mingling with hers. I was going to come, couldn't stop it, didn't want to stop it. "Please tell me you're ready."

"I'm ready."

To make sure, I slid a finger between us, giving her some extra attention.

"Oh God. Keep doing that. Don't stop."

I didn't stop.

"Nick. Oh, Nick." She stiffened, straining out her release.

"Right here, baby. Let me have it. All of it." I kept on moving, in and out, my own orgasm building, strengthening, until holy fucking shit…

The world stopped. Time stopped. My heart stopped… okay, no they didn't, but they could have, as far as I was concerned…at least for a few seconds. My body completely spent, I collapsed on top of Leigh, sweating, practically gasping for breath. "So fucking good."

She hugged me and kissed the side of my head as I succumbed to the aftermath of pure, unadulterated pleasure.

At some point Leigh tried to slide out from under me. "Wait." I grabbed the condom and pulled out of her.

She turned away, reaching for her clothes, not looking at me.

Not good.

"Hey," I said. "What's wrong?"

"I'm not…" She shrugged. "I don't usually…"

"Listen, you showed me yours and I showed you mine. We just had us some extremely hot, extremely satisfying sex. No regrets." I leaned in and kissed her lower back. "No nerves. No embarrassment. Got it?"

She flashed me a little smile and nodded. “We did just have us some extremely hot, extremely satisfying sex, didn’t we?” She looked rather proud of that fact.

“We most certainly did.” I found my shorts and slipped them on. “Now point me to the bathroom.”

“Inside to the left, just after the kitchen.”

I walked in that direction. “When I come back, it’s my turn to lotion *you* up,” I said over my shoulder. “You’re starting to turn pink.”

On my way past my bag, I grabbed another condom, in anticipation of round two.

Chapter Ten

Leigh

Toward the end of our third week together, Nick got us into a charming restaurant with stunning views of Sag Harbor Bay. "I love looking at the water." Always had, ever since I was a child. "It's so relaxing."

"You've never been here during a hurricane," Nick said, buttering a roll.

My stomach tightened at the thought of all that water churning about. I tore a roll in half and took a bite. "I'm sorry about yesterday," when I'd thrown up over the side of the boat that'd taken us out for parasailing.

Nick reached for my hand and gave it a squeeze. "Like I told you then, it's no big deal. I've gone parasailing before, and I'll go parasailing again."

Pretty sure the five other people on board hadn't felt the

same way. "Thank you." I wasn't typically prone to motion sickness, although I had suffered the occasional roller coaster-induced nausea in the past. Up until yesterday, boating had never bothered me. Not a good sign.

A cute little blond waitress's arrival at our table stopped my thoughts from plummeting into pregnancy paranoia. "My name's Ashley. I'll be your server this evening. Can I start you off with a drink?"

If only. "Just water for me," I told her.

She turned to Nick.

"Water for me, too."

When she left, I said, "Just because I'm not drinking alcohol doesn't mean you can't. I'm happy to serve as your designated driver."

"Take it as a compliment." He set down his roll. "Lately, before the summer, that is, most of my dates have required a pre-pickup beer primer and a two-drink minimum for me to tolerate them through dinner. But with you," he leaned in, resting one elbow on the table, "no alcohol buzz required for me to enjoy your company."

He had a way of warming me down to my soul. I smiled. "Thank you." This time I reached for *his* hand, but rather than squeezing it, I held on. "I enjoy spending time with you, too. No alcohol buzz required for me, either." Which was a good thing, considering…

He smiled back. "Last night, while you were out with your friends, I told Murphy I got laid off."

I'd been wondering about that. "How'd it go?"

"He's gone into crisis mode. Starting today, we're

economizing." Nick took a sip of water. "He's clipping coupons and wants to start planning meals around weekly specials at the grocery store. Do you know what's on sale this week? Rump roast. What the hell is a rump roast? The name doesn't generate a nice visual, I'll tell you that."

I laughed.

"And he's considering exchanging all the light bulbs in the house for energy saving sixty watt bulbs and cutting back to basic cable."

"Oh the horror," I teased.

"Desperate times," Nick teased back. "Even though I have assured him we are far from desperate. Today he rallied his friends for an emergency meeting at the house. Before I left I heard talk of a multi-family yard sale, to be held in the parking lot of the senior center, to give each of them a chance to raise some money. Someone's got a son who owns a hot dog cart. Someone's granddaughter can do face painting. There's going to be kettle corn and a blow up slide for the kids."

"I think it's a wonderful idea. It'll give him something to do."

"Give *him* something to do?" Nick stared at me. "Who do you think is going to wind up crawling around in the attic? Me. Who do you think is going to have to drag stuff up from the basement? Me. Who do you think is going to have to haul all of Murphy's junk to the senior center? Me."

"You're a good grandson." I patted his hand.

"Not really," he said, shifting his gaze to my lips. "All I want to do is ditch the old man so I can spend all of my time with you." He reached out to where I sat on his left, cupped the back of my neck, and tugged me close. His mouth touching my ear, he whispered, "Alone." He let out a hot, moist breath that shot tingles throughout my body. "Preferably naked."

Sometimes his words warmed me down to my soul. Other times, they warmed other places. Since our first time together, I'd started to crave Nick's touch. I loved the closeness we'd shared, more than once, and wanted more of it. At this point, the mere mention of 'preferably naked,' in that sexy tone of his, had me ready to actually get naked, with him, someplace more private. "Do you think we can get our meals to go?"

Nick sat back, pointing. "And miss that?"

I turned to see the most beautiful sunset, the sky ablaze with vibrant oranges, reds and purples, the sun reflecting on the water as it lowered into the horizon.

Nick held my hand as we both watched, the restaurant near silent as others enjoyed nature's beauty with us.

It was as if Ashley waited for the exact moment the sun disappeared to come and take our orders.

After she left, Nick shifted in his seat and rubbed his free hand around the back of his neck, like he seemed to do whenever something was bothering him. "As much as I want to spend all of my time with you, clothes on *or* off," he gave me a little smile. "And as much as I didn't want my job search to impact our 'Summer of Fun,' I think I need to go on a few interviews, if for no other reason than to put Murphy's mind at ease and show him there are employers out there interested in hiring me."

"Of course."

"So you won't be mad if I have to head into the city for a day or two?"

I shook my head. He didn't get mad whenever I headed to Westchester. "Let me know when, and if I don't have any plans with Storme or Kelsey, and my dad is free, I'll go home on those days."

What followed was the best dinner date I'd ever had with a man close to my own age. Conversation flowed easily. I enjoyed watching Nick talk, so animated when he told a funny story, so sincere when discussing his grandmother, his love for his grandparents as evident as his frustration with his parents for leaving the area and basically washing their hands of Murphy since he'd refused to move with them.

After dinner, as with every other evening we'd spent together over the past week or so, Nick and I ended up taking a stroll on the beach, shoes off, hand in hand.

"You're awfully quiet tonight," I noted as a wave rolled in, the deepest part hitting me mid-calf.

"Thinking," was all he said.

"About what?" Remembering those fish that'd slithered around my feet on our first beach walk, I switched positions so he'd be the one to walk in the deeper water.

"A woman."

A woman, huh? "Tell me about her."

"She's about five-feet-six or seven inches tall, has light brownish-reddish hair, and a great figure."

I was five-feet-six-and-a-half inches tall with light brownish-reddish hair. "Her looks are all that matter to you?"

"She's also sweet, kind and forgiving." He brought my hand up to his lips and kissed it.

"She sounds boring."

"Not boring at all. She's fun and likes to play in the water, which I like to do, too. She's smart and very sexy. But even more important, she has a high level of tolerance for a certain senior citizen who loves chocolate cake and television game shows."

I bumped my shoulder into his. "Murphy is a great guy." I brought Nick's hand up to mine and kissed it. "Like his grandson."

We continued on in silence.

When it had gone on long enough, in my opinion, I asked, "So what has you so deep in thought about this particular woman?"

"I want to ask her something, but I'm not sure exactly how to go about it."

I took two quick steps, turned, and jumped in front of him. "You mean she's so difficult to talk to, you don't feel comfortable just coming out and asking?"

He shook his head as his hands landed on my hips and pulled me close. "I'm worried she may think it's too soon. We haven't known each other very long."

Too soon for what? We'd already had sex twice, once on the pool float and a second time, earlier this week, against the side of Murphy's house. It'd happened when Nick had walked me out to say goodbye after another family barbecue. In the dark, gentle kisses had turned hungry and fierce. The next thing I knew my back was being slammed up against the vinyl siding and I was wrapping my legs around his waist, our movements frantic, our desire for one another out of control. It'd been the best sex of my life. "Maybe she won't." I leaned in, loosely wrapping my arms around his back. "Maybe she wants what you want." More.

"She'll worry about what my granddad will think, which is one of the reasons I like her so much, by the way."

"Just ask."

"Leigh."

"Yes." To anything. Everything.

"I'd like to—"

"Yes."

He nuzzled against my ear. I could feel his smile. "...spend the night with you, the whole night, in your bed."

A flare of arousal shot through my system at the suggestion, arousal and something else...something good that I couldn't identify. In such a short time, he knew me so well. Under normal circumstances I *would* have been concerned about Murphy's opinion of me, knowing Nick had spent the night. But right then, I wanted Nick more than I wanted Murphy to think highly of me. Before I could convince myself to say, 'No,' I said, "Yes."

I didn't remember the walk back to Storme's house, only that I felt winded by the time we reached the stairs to her lower deck. While hurrying along, in the glow from the pool, I saw Kelsey and Sean making out on a lounge chair.

They didn't notice us.

We didn't stop to chat.

In my room, I flicked on the light while Nick closed and locked the door.

"Tonight we take it slow," he said, as he turned and walked toward me, his voice deep and seductive. "I'm going to take my time." He slid his hands to my butt and squeezed, smoothed them up my sides, lifting my shirt, skimming over my ribs to my breasts. "Explore every inch of you." He pressed his hips against mine, the bulge of his arousal hitting most pleasurably between my legs.

I loved the feel of his hands on me, so confident and skilled, knowing just what I liked and where I liked it. He undid the front clasp of my bra, sliding both hands beneath it, rubbing his knuckles over my nipples.

I couldn't contain a groan. "God, I like that."

"You like this even more." In one swift movement he removed my shirt and my bra and put his mouth on me, sucking my right nipple…hard.

Sooooo goooood. No joke, I literally thought my knees might give out from the overwhelming intensity of the yearning coursing through my body. I grabbed on to Nick's shoulders to hold myself up as he moved over to my other nipple.

Eyes closed, my head dropped back, and I groaned again. "If your plan is to take things slow, you might want to stop doing that."

He laughed against my skin, a deep, rich, decadent sound. A cocky kind of laugh that had me dropping to my knees to show him I could push him toward losing control just as easily as he could push me.

Before he could stop me, I shoved my hand up the inside of his leg beneath his cargo shorts and cupped his hot, hard length through the cotton of his briefs.

He let out a breath and opened his thighs to give me room.

I caressed him up and down, firmly, looking up, watching him as I did. "You like that?"

He tilted his head down. "Baby, you know I love having your hands on me."

Interesting. No one had ever called me 'baby' during sex before. I kind of liked it. "Only my hands?" I asked, using them to unbutton and unzip. "What about other parts of me?" I lowered the elastic of his black cotton briefs, exposing him. "Like my cheek for instance." I rubbed my cheek against his oh so smooth skin. "Or my tongue?" I swirled the tip of my tongue around the tip of him, tasting him for the first time. "Or my mouth?" I took him deep.

"Shit, Leigh." He grabbed onto the dresser by the door to steady himself.

I didn't stop, sucking him deep again and again, one hand moving in tandem with my mouth, the other cupping his balls.

Now it was his turn to groan, a gratifying sound if ever I'd heard one.

"You still want to take things slow?" I teased, standing up so I could wrap my arms around his neck and kiss him on the mouth.

He kissed me like he was a man minutes away from dying and my lips contained the power to save him. I kissed him back with a need, a hunger I feared would never be satisfied.

When we came up for air, he stripped off his shirt. My skirt and panties were the next to go.

Not wanting to be the only one standing naked in a fully lit room, I lowered his shorts and briefs until they fell to the floor and he kicked them aside.

"Give me ten seconds, then turn off the lights," I told him.

I turned to find the candle and matches by the bed, igniting the flame just in time to keep the room from being plunged into darkness.

"Where were we?" Nick pressed his naked front to my naked back, cupping my breasts and kissing my neck as he did.

I tilted my head to give him full access. "I recall mention of you exploring every inch of me." Every inch of me practically vibrated with gleeful anticipation.

"You seem to like that idea." He steered me toward the bed.

"I do."

"Lay down."

I did.

Good Lord, the man had skills, taking his time, using his lips and his tongue, his fingers, his legs and feet. My neck tingled, my nipples hardened, and the needy place between my legs throbbed for attention, unwilling to wait. "Please." I rocked my hips, needing more. "Later." I needed him so bad. "You can explore every inch of me later." I tried to pull him on top of me.

"Wait," he said. "Condom."

Thank goodness one of us was thinking clearly. Condom on, Nick crawled up my body, oh so slowly, and settled himself between my legs.

I opened wider to make room for him. "Finally," I teased.

Holding himself up on straight arms, Nick looked down, watching me as he slid inside, taking his time, moving forward, a little bit, then back, forward then back, inch by inch, stretching me, filling me, his eyes never leaving mine.

I reached up to play with his nipples. They hardened but didn't distract Nick from his task as he continued his slow, sensual glide, all the way in, all the way out, again and again. So focused. So intense. So controlled.

So different from the last two times we'd been together, his movements and expression filled with caring. I remembered a conversation from one of our moonlit walks on the beach.

I'd asked, *"You'd waste your one wish on having sex with me?"*

He'd answered, *"It wouldn't be a waste…and it wouldn't be just sex."*

Tonight didn't feel like 'just sex.' My heart swelled, because tonight he was purposely taking his time, making love to me. As much as I appreciated it and loved him for it, I wanted more, wanted him crazy with lust, on the verge of losing it, desperate for release. I contracted my internal muscles, squeezing him tight as I shot my hips up to meet him.

He faltered the tiniest bit.

"Faster." I lifted my legs, crossing them behind his back, my feet at his butt, trying to force him to increase his pace.

It didn't work.

"Harder." I raked my fingers up his sides and clamped my hands behind his back, trying to pull his full weight on top of me.

It didn't work.

"Please." I writhed beneath him, trying to reposition, to feel... "I need…"

I don't know if it was my begging tone or if he needed what I needed, but Nick dropped on top of me, gathered me into his arms, and fucked me. While I hated that word, and would never say it out loud, there was no other way to describe it. He plunged deep, again and again, angling his hips, moving like a wild man. "Yes." I loved it. "More."

"You feel so fucking good," he said. "God help me." He kissed my ear, my cheek and chin.

As my orgasm started to build, I set my feet on the bed and, knees bent, drove my hips up, swiveled them.

Nick groaned, his breathing heavy, his body slick with sweat.

"Oh God." So close. So amazingly good. "I'm…." was all I could get out before my orgasm slammed into me and out of me. Spectacular.

"Shit." Nick stiffened above me. Then he pulled out, pushed back in, and stiffened again. "Fuck." He let out a groan.

I smiled.

He went limp on top of me. I loved the feel of him, his body spent, exhausted, and, I hoped, as satisfied as mine.

I thought he'd fallen asleep, but all too soon he shifted off of me, and with a, "be right back," he left the bed and went into the bathroom.

When he returned, he climbed in behind me, still wonderfully naked, gathering me into his arms and cuddling in close.

I'd never gone to sleep, in my bed, in the arms of a naked man before. I'd never felt like I was falling in love with a man before…tonight. The thought that I may be falling in love with Nick made my heart ache with regret. *Children ruin everything*, he'd said, making his opinion clear. I had no future with a man who didn't want children, because in a few months, more likely than not, I'd be having one.

Chapter Eleven

Nick

Five days after my dinner date with Leigh, and the absolute best night I'd ever spent with a woman, I sat in the upscale lobby of The DeGray Group, waiting for my interview, the second of the day, staring at the indoor waterfall, hating smelly cabs and crowded Manhattan streets and all the clothing required for me to look professional.

I missed the beach.

I missed Leigh. Four weeks into our 'Summer of Fun' and I didn't want our time together to end.

"Mr. Kenzy."

A very distinguished older gentleman, maybe mid to late fifties, with a full head of thick, salt and pepper colored hair, walked toward me. He wore an expensive-looking, dark gray suit, a bright white dress shirt, and a perfectly tied red silk tie. He held out his hand to me.

"Yes." I picked up my briefcase, stood and shook the man's hand.

"Garrett DeGray," he said.

I nearly swallowed my tongue.

Garrett DeGray? The head of The DeGray Group? One of the most successful fund managers of the past decade, averaging a return of 12.6% over the past five years? That Garrett DeGray?

He smiled. It caught me off guard, because it almost looked familiar, although I had no idea why. I'd never met the man, had never even seen his picture, but everyone in the business knew of his successes.

"I'm sorry, sir," I said, trying to regroup. "I thought I'd be meeting with someone from the Human Resources department, not the man in charge."

"I had some time available," he said matter-of-factly. "Come." He turned, obviously used to giving a command and having it followed. While I walked, I noticed he was cordial to his staff, recognizing some by name, others with a nod of his head. People moved out of his way, in my estimation, more out of respect than of fear.

He took me to a boardroom on the main floor rather than his office. With the two of us closed inside, he said, "My daughter thinks very highly of you, and she is a very good judge of character." He walked to a narrow table along the wall, picked up a pitcher, and poured himself a glass of water. He held it up. "Would you like a drink?"

No. I wanted answers. "I'm sorry, sir. Your daughter?"

He poured a second glass and handed it to me.

I gulped it down like I'd just finished a marathon, having some difficulty coming to terms with the fact I was alone in a room with Garrett DeGray, the man every Wall Street analyst, myself included, dreamed of one day becoming. For some reason, though, he thought I knew his daughter. I didn't. Which meant this entire meeting was a mistake.

My excitement at learning The DeGray Group was hiring at the same time I found myself in need of a job turned to instant regret.

Mr. DeGray sat down at the head of the table and motioned to the seat on his right. I sat.

"I'm sorry, sir," I said again. "I think there's been some type of mistake." Much to my overwhelming disappointment. I should have known this interview was too good to be true.

He gave me that oddly familiar smile again. Then he clasped his fingers together and set them on the table in front of him. "I see she didn't tell you who she is, which doesn't surprise me."

Didn't tell me who she is? Who didn't tell me who she is?

"My daughter insists on getting by on her own merit. One of the many things I admire about her, in addition to her being smart, loving, and an exceptional judge of character, which I believe I already mentioned."

I sat there trying to follow along while not letting my confusion show.

"Leigh," he said. "My daughter is Leigh. You met her in the Hamptons."

Thank the good Lord I was sitting down. I'd done a hell of a lot more than simply meet her in the Hamptons. The things I'd been doing with this man's daughter over the past few weeks. I felt my face heat. The things I still wanted to do before the end of the summer.

If I were Leigh's father, I'd shoot me.

He smiled again. "I think she feels the same way about you."

If she did, then why hadn't she been honest about who she really was? "So exactly why am I here?" I couldn't help but ask. "Did Leigh ask you to meet with me?" Did she think I wasn't capable of finding my own job?

"No," he said firmly. "She's been spending a lot of time talking about you. It's not like Leigh to go on and on about a man." Mr. DeGray studied me as if trying to identify my appeal. "When she mentioned you'd worked as an analyst on Wall Street for the past two years and were currently looking for a new job, I had my director of human resources call around to find out which headhunters you were working with to get you in here for an interview before some other company snapped you up. I'm always on the hunt for good people."

Ahhh. To be snapped up by another company so quickly and easily.

"So there's really a job?" I asked. "This isn't some father recon to find out more about the man currently dating his daughter?" I didn't add, 'For the summer' because that made our relationship sound cheap and meaningless, and it wasn't, at least not to me.

Mr. DeGray smiled again. I saw Leigh in that smile. "I guess it's a little of both, Mr. Kenzy."

"Please, call me Nick."

"Nick." Mr. DeGray took a sip of water, then stared

thoughtfully into the glass. "Leigh is the most important person in my world, Nick. As much as I wish she'd taken a job here at my company, I respect her for wanting to earn her success on her own, unencumbered by a father's protection and whispers of nepotism. But I do hope that one day she'll join me…join us," he looked me in the eyes. "If it turns out you're the right man for the position I'm looking to fill."

I couldn't help but wonder about the exact nature of the position Leigh's father was looking to fill.

Needless to say, on the train ride back to the Hamptons, I had a lot to think about.

By the time Leigh came over for dinner that night, I was having a hard time controlling my anger. She'd lied to me about who she was. Maybe not outright, but a lie of omission was just the same, in my book. We'd welcomed her into Murphy's small, somewhat rundown home. Leigh DeGray, daughter of a billionaire fund manager, slumming it.

What did a man like me have to offer a woman like her…besides sex? Nothing she couldn't buy for herself, that was for sure. That made me even angrier. At some point, my subconscious had started to think of our relationship as more than a summer fling. At some point, my heart had gotten involved. And now my heart hurt.

Leigh was perfect for me.

Or so I'd thought.

Now, every time she smiled at my granddad or enthusiastically encouraged him about his plans for the huge, and growing-by-the-day, yard sale, I wanted to scream, "Stop patronizing his paltry attempt to raise money! What do you know about needing money?" Every time she smiled at me or touched my arm, or made some other familiar, caring gesture, I wanted to scream, "Stop pretending to like me or care about me! All you want me for is sex." And didn't that feel shitty? Call me petty, but I wanted to make her feel as shitty as learning the truth had made me feel.

But not in front of my granddad, which meant I had to wait for Jeopardy to start before I could confront her.

Finally! As Murphy carefully closed the screened door behind him, I swallowed down my second beer, trying to remain outwardly calm. Inside I felt anything but calm.

"Are you okay?" Leigh asked, looking concerned. "I know I promised not to ask you about your job search, but did something happen today?"

Damn right something happened today. "What's your last name?"

Confusion showed on her face. "My last name? Why?"

"I want to know." I sat back, casually resting one elbow on the arm of the deck chair, my impersonation of a completely relaxed male. "Indulge me. Please."

"DeGray," she said matter-of-factly, like it was no big deal.

"DeGray as in 'The DeGray Fund' DeGray?" I found sitting back and faking calm didn't work for me, so I sat up then, hell, I stood, could not sit one second longer. "DeGray as in Garrett DeGray's daughter?"

Leigh stood too, only hesitantly. "What's wrong, Nick?"

"Do Storme and Kelsey know?" Or had she been lying to them, too?

She let out a breath. "They know my father works on Wall

Street but, as far as I know, they have no idea how successful he is. I doubt they'd care, even if they did."

"Why didn't you tell *me*?" I asked.

"I don't typically tell people my last name because I don't want to be thought of as a rich, snobby, pardon the term, bitch, because I'm not."

No. She wasn't.

"And what do you think," she went on, "would have happened if I had told you, a Wall Street analyst, my name? Would you have come to apologize to me at the bonfire? Would you have invited me to your grandfather's house for dinner? Would we have what we have now if you had known who my father was?"

No, we most likely would not have what we have now if I'd known who her father was. I would have realized she was too far out of my league and stayed the hell away from her.

"It shouldn't even matter."

"Of course if matters. Your father is a billionaire. You're rich. Richer than rich. I don't even know the correct word to describe what you are."

"No," Leigh said calmly as she walked to the railing beside me and looked out over the garden. "My father has a lot of money, but it's his money not mine. He's not an extravagant spender. We live a simple life."

"You drive a Subaru!"

"Yes, I do." She looked at me like I was crazy. "It's a dependable car."

So damn practical.

"What happened that's got you so upset?" she asked quietly.

I turned to face her, crossing my arms over my chest in the process. "I had an interview today. At The DeGray Group. Imagine my surprise when your dad knew all about me."

"My dad interviewed you?"

"Surprised me, too." It'd damn near shocked the shit out of me. "Apparently you've been talking about me, which is very unlike you." I should have been flattered, but I was too pissed off.

She blushed, and that softened my anger a bit.

"So daddy wanted to check me out," I told her, "and had his director of HR contact a few head hunters until he found one I'm working with."

"And he interviewed you *himself*?"

I nodded.

"I swear," Leigh said, with her hand over her heart, "I didn't put him up to it. I didn't know anything about it. I promise you."

"I know." At least I knew for sure as of that moment, because the sincerity of her tone and the look on her face told me the truth.

"Did he offer you a job?"

"Would it matter if he did?"

She looked away.

That gave me my answer. I asked again anyway. "Leigh? Would it matter if he did?"

She stared into the backyard, avoiding me. "I'd never stand in the way of you taking a job at my dad's company." An ant crawled toward her on the old wood railing, and she brushed it over the side. "It'd be a wonderful opportunity for you. He gets hundreds of applications a month, from all over the country."

I could almost hear the 'but' in her voice, so I gave her a prompt. "But..."

She turned to face me. "But...nothing. If he offered you a job and you want the job, take it," she glanced into the backyard, "as long as you're okay with seeing me...after."

After we were over, like there was no doubt in her mind that when the summer ended our relationship would end, too.

"Just so you know," she continued. "Whenever I can, I stop by to see him at work. I attend all of his holiday parties and some business functions. Plus, I'm on his board of directors..."

"Wait." What? "You're on his board of directors?" Unbelievable.

She nodded. "Since I turned eighteen. Dad wants me involved so I know what's going on in his company. In case anything happens to him...In case I have to..." She inhaled a shaky breath, and I could tell just how much losing her father worried her.

Just like that, my anger dissipated. Suddenly, comforting Leigh took priority. My feelings of inadequacy no longer mattered...for the time being. "Hey," I said quietly, reaching out to touch her chin, to make her look at me. "When I saw your father, he looked fine."

"He's not. He works too hard, needs to slow down, but he won't." She tried to look away. I didn't let her.

"Come here." I opened my arms.

She stepped into my embrace, so vulnerable, and I held her. "You know, no matter what happens at the end of the summer, I'll always be here for you if you need me. For any reason."

Stupid idiot that I was, I wanted to take care of her and protect her and help her in any way I could. *Like helping her run her father's multi-billion dollar company if, God forbid, the need should arise?* Yes, if that's what she needed. Only how would she look at his offer to extend their relationship past the end of the summer, now that she knew that he knew who her father was?

Chapter Twelve

Leigh

I came awake slowly, lying on my left side. I inhaled the cool, ocean-scented night air and listened to the waves crashing into the shore nearby. A body pressed in behind me. Strong arms held me close.

Nick.

Six weeks together, and I hated to think about saying goodbye to him, about living the rest of my life without him in it.

"You're awake," he said quietly.

I nodded, opening my eyes to see we were together on a padded lounge chair by the pool at Storme's house. "I'm sorry. I fell asleep on you again." That made four nights in a row. Each time, I'd woken up in Nick's arms.

He kissed my hair. "You've worked hard this week."

Yes, I had, but so had he and Murphy. We'd all put in dozens of hours at his granddad's house, going through every closet and drawer, every cabinet and box, sorting out things to keep, to sell, and to throw away. He'd had A LOT of stuff crammed into that small house.

"I can't believe we pulled it off in only three weeks," Nick said. "And that it was such a success," he kissed me again, "thanks to you."

With word of mouth, Murphy's yard sale had grown into a full-fledged flea market. "Your granddad and his friends put everything together." They'd coordinated the location, the vendors, forty-two of them, and the permits. "As a public relations professional, publicity is part of what I do." With a little creative sign-making help from Kelsey – using key words like 'vintage,' 'antique,' and 'fun for the kids,' — and strategic posting of said signs by Storme, who had lots of connections in the area. Plus, I'd taken out ads in two local newspapers and, after some research, set up Murphy and Nick to record two different radio ads at two different radio stations, each to appeal to a specific demographic.

"You got hundreds of people to show up on Saturday *and* Sunday."

"I didn't do it alone, and the cloudy days helped."

"Well, thank you." He hugged me tightly from behind.

"You're welcome." I rubbed my bare feet along his hairy calves.

"Murphy figures he made over three thousand dollars."

"That's great. Hopefully it will ease his imagined money worries for the time being."

"I think his money worries eased when I told him I'd been offered two jobs," Nick said.

"Two? That's fantastic!" I waited for him to provide more information.

He didn't.

"Last I spoke to him, Murphy was trying to decide between hopping a bus to Atlantic City, hiding his bundle of bills in the freezer, or putting the money into the bank. I got the feeling he was leaning toward Atlantic City."

I turned in Nick's arms, laughing as I did. "You have got to be kidding me! After all that work he's going to blow his money on blackjack and slot machines?"

Nick smiled, so handsome in the moonlight…in any light, for that matter. "No. He's planning to *double* his money on blackjack and slot machines."

I shook my head. "Well, it's his to do with as he chooses."

Nick looked deeply into my eyes as he smoothed his thumb along my cheek. "You really went all out for us." He kissed my forehead. "I promised you a 'Summer of Fun.' This past week wasn't very fun."

"Yes it was." Exhausting but fun. "I enjoyed spending time with you and Murphy, going through his pictures and mementos from years past, and listening to his stories."

"That man sure can talk."

Yes. He could. But I didn't mind. "He gave me a beautiful brooch that belonged to his mother and a vintage handbag and silver bangle bracelet that belonged to Lilly." I'd tried to turn them down, but he wouldn't let me.

"He really likes you." Nick kissed the tip of my nose. "So

do I." He slid his lips down to meet mine, so gentle and caring.

I smiled. "I like you, too, Nick." So much. I could be myself around him, without feeling like I had to go out of my way to impress him. I could be quiet around him, without feeling like I had to fill the silence with conversation. I felt comfortable around him...happy…content. I hugged him.

"What was that for?"

"No reason." I shifted to my back to look up at the stars in the sky, resting my head on Nick's upper arm. "Remember how you asked me if I had one wish, what I'd wish for?"

He nodded.

"It pains me to admit that I would selfishly wish this summer didn't have to end. That you and I could stay here in the Hamptons, together, just as we are tonight, forever."

"I like that wish." He took my hand into his and rested them on my slightly rounded belly. "If only I had the power to grant it."

If only. "Two weeks left." Until he went back to his life and I went back to mine.

"You know we could—"

"Don't." I reached up and put my finger to his lips, couldn't bear to hear what he had to say. There was no future for us. While I had yet to take a pregnancy test, I could see and feel the changes in my body, knew what they meant. I wouldn't saddle Nick with a wife and a baby that wasn't his, an instant family he didn't want or deserve.

"But—" he tried.

"Please don't." I cut him off, feeling tears gathering in my eyes. "Kiss me." I grabbed his T-shirt and pulled his upper body on top of me. When his lips touched mine, worry, sadness and dread disappeared. When his hands caressed my body, I felt beautiful and sexy and desirable. "Make love to me." *Give me memories I will treasure forever.*

And right there, beneath the starry sky, by the side of the pool, he did.

Chapter THIRTEEN

Nick

Two days.

I hadn't seen or heard from Leigh in two whole days, despite sending her dozens of texts and snap chats and leaving a bunch of messages on her voicemail.

Just before noon on what would be day three, I steered my car into Storme's driveway, knowing something was wrong.

Upon seeing Leigh's two friends arguing up by the garage, Storme carrying a suitcase, I could tell my suspicions were correct. When they saw me, they froze.

I parked and got out of my car. "Hello ladies."

Silence.

"Leigh around?" I asked.

Storme glanced at Kelsey, who answered, "No." With Kelsey's attention on me, Storme threw her suitcase in the back seat of her convertible, then went to open the driver's side door.

"No," Kelsey said, rushing the few steps to lean against it, holding it closed. "Leigh doesn't want us there."

"Doesn't want you where?" I asked.

They ignored me.

"She needs us," Storme said. "Especially now."

Why especially now? I got a sick feeling in my gut.

"If she wanted us to go with her, she wouldn't have snuck out of here before dawn," Kelsey said. "She wouldn't have left us a note specifically telling us not to follow her."

Storme looked down and wiped an eye. "I feel terrible."

Kelsey hugged her. "Leigh is the strongest, smartest, most together person I know. She'll figure it out. She needs some time alone. You know how she gets."

"She's always been there for me," Storme said, turning to the car. "I need to be there for her."

"You need to come back inside and calm down," Kelsey said. "Your parents and your fiancé will be here soon, and you can't go running up to Westchester. There's too much to for the wedding. Leigh understands."

It was like they'd forgotten all about me. I cleared my throat. When they looked over, I waved. "Remember me?"

"She won't want you there, either," Kelsey said.

"Especially not you," Storme added.

"Why?" I asked, possibilities already percolating in my mind, none of them good. "And where is she?"

"Home," Storme said.

"Storme," Kelsey cautioned.

Since it seemed I'd have more luck with Storme than Kelsey,

I focused on her. "Why did she go home?"

Storme glanced at Kelsey. "Her grandfather passed away."

Shit. "When?"

"She must have gotten the call late last night." Storme wiped at the corner of her eye. "She went to bed around nine. When we woke up, she was gone."

"But that doesn't explain why I haven't heard from her for the last two days," I said.

Storme wouldn't look at me.

Kelsey looked me straight in the eye but said nothing.

"Please," was all I could think to say. Then I stood there, waiting, hoping one of them would take pity on me and tell me what was going on.

It didn't take Storme long. "She's—"

"Don't," Kelsey cut her off. "If Leigh wanted him to know, she would have told him."

I wanted to ask 'Know what?' but decided to keep quiet to see what would happen next.

Slamming her hands on her hips, Storme stood up to Kelsey. "I know Leigh said she needed time and she didn't want either of us to go after her, but she didn't say anything about Nick."

"Because he's not supposed to know," Kelsey argued.

"She's got too much going on," Storme argued back. "All this stress can't be good for the baby."

Kelsey's eyes went wide.

Storme sucked in a breath.

The news didn't come as a surprise. As much as I'd hoped she wasn't, I'd seen the signs. "She took a test?" I asked, my heart starting to race on Leigh's behalf, thinking about what she must be going through right now.

Kelsey nodded. "I woke up to her vomiting in the bathroom early Monday morning."

Two days ago.

"We knew something was going on, even before that," Storme said. "She was quieter than usual, always daydreaming."

"She wasn't drinking like she usually does."

"Not that she's a big drinker," Storme said. "But she does love my family's wine."

"She refused potato chips," Kelsey added.

"Told me she was worried about fitting into her dress for the wedding," Storme said. "And she'd started eating yogurt and drinking milk."

"I ran out to the pharmacy and bought a test," Kelsey said. "We stood outside the bathroom door until she took it."

"Then we all cried when it turned out to be positive." Storme wiped at her eye again. "I've never seen her so unhappy. Now, on top of that, she has to say goodbye to her grandpa, who helped raise her. And you know she'll be worrying about her dad's heart and how she's going to tell him."

I'd heard enough. "What's her dad's address?" I took out my phone, ready to plug it into my GPS.

Neither one answered. "I agree with Storme," I told them. "Leigh's got too much going on to deal with it all on her own. She needs someone to lean on. Let me be the one to go after her." I stared directly at Storme. "Please." When she just stood there looking at me, trying to decide, I added, "I love her." I hadn't planned for it to happen, but it had.

Four hours later, the GPS guided me into an upscale neighborhood in Harrison, New York, one of the wealthiest suburbs in Westchester County. I passed by several large homes with perfectly manicured lawns and gardens before I found number twelve on my right and pulled into a long paved driveway.

The two-story red brick house, with interesting architecture and lots of windows, could easily have graced the cover of a magazine, yet it didn't scream, 'A billionaire lives here.' I drove up to the four car garage and parked beside Leigh's Subaru.

A minute later I rang the bell, my heart pounding, not sure who would answer the door or what type of reception I'd receive. The only thing I *was* sure of was that I had to come, had to at least try to console her.

Leigh answered the door, wearing a simple black dress and simple black heels, her eyes red and puffy, and my heart broke. She didn't look surprised to see me and said nothing as she stepped aside to let me in. After she closed the door, she said, "Kelsey called to tell me you were on the way. I tried to call you but—"

"I didn't answer. Nothing you could have said would have stopped me from coming." I walked toward her. "I'm so sorry to hear about your grandfather." I gave her a hug. She stood stiffly and didn't hug me back, not at all like the warm, affectionate Leigh I'd been dating for more than six weeks. A bad sign. I released her.

"We just got home from my grandfather's memorial service."

"So soon?"

"Dad wanted it done right away, so like he always does, he made it happen." She dabbed at her eye with a tissue. "My grandfather's body will be cremated later today."

The doorbell rang. "Damn it. I told him to stay in the car until I could—"

Leigh opened the door and there stood Murphy, holding the fruit basket he'd insisted I stop to get after he'd insisted on coming with me.

"Murphy!" Leigh took the fruit basket and thrust it in my direction. "I'm so glad you came." Then she threw herself into my granddad's arms and sobbed harder than I'd ever seen a woman cry in my life.

"There, there." Murphy patted her back while he looked over her shoulder and gave me one of his, 'I told you so' looks.

Fine. He'd been right. Again.

Garrett DeGray walked into the entryway, wearing a dark gray suit, asking, "Who's at the door?"

"Mr. DeGray." I held out my hand. "I'm so sorry for your loss."

"In my home, it's Garrett." He shook my hand, his grip firm, glancing toward Leigh and my granddad, then back at me.

"That's my grandfather, Murphy Kenzy," I explained. "He and Leigh have grown close over the past few weeks. He insisted on coming with me."

Murphy held out a hand, Leigh still clinging to him, crying. "Nice to meet you."

Garrett shook his hand. "Please. Come in. Leigh, let Murphy move." He turned back to me. "She and her grandfather were very close. She's taking his passing very hard." He looked at his daughter with concern and quietly added, "I've never seen her this upset. Not even after her mother died."

Leigh stepped away from Murphy, wiping her eyes, still sniffling. "I'm sorry." She took the fruit basket, not making eye contact with any of us. "Thank you for your thoughtful gift. You've had a long drive. Please come in." We followed her to a nice, very upscale sitting room. "Make yourselves comfortable. The bathroom is down the hall on the right." She pointed. "I'll go pour us some iced tea." Then she turned and left the room.

Typical Leigh, striving to do the right thing and take care of others, but she didn't have to, not today, not for Murphy and me. "I'll go help," I told Garrett, following after her.

I found Leigh in the huge, modern kitchen, with lots of black and lots of chrome, holding on to the handle of a huge black refrigerator, staring down at the speckled marble countertop, motionless.

I walked up behind her. "You don't have to wait on us."

She turned, slowly, looking so sad, so lost. I opened my arms and she stepped into them, setting her head to my shoulder. I hugged her tightly. This time she hugged me back. "I know it sounds trite, but everything really is going to be okay."

She nodded. "At some point. But right now…" She inhaled a shuddery breath, then let it out. "Right now it doesn't feel that way." We stood there for a few minutes. It was as if I could feel her body relaxing in my arms. It felt good.

"Storme told you," she said.

"That you're pregnant? Yes."

"That you're what?" Garrett DeGray bellowed. "Pregnant?" He grabbed onto the island counter with one hand and clutched his chest with the other.

"Daddy!" Leigh ran toward him. "Where are your pills?"

He fumbled in the pocket of his suit jacket and handed her a small prescription bottle.

She quickly opened it and handed him the medicine, and he slipped it under his tongue.

Murphy smacked the back of my head. "Nicholas Vincent Kenzy, your parents raised you better than that. Of all the stupid, irresponsible—"

"The baby isn't his," Leigh said, helping her father onto a stool.

"But you two..." Murphy said, looking between me and Leigh.

She undid her dad's tie and unbuttoned the top button of his dress shirt. "It happened before we met."

"She told me she might be pregnant before we started dating," I added.

"And you dated her anyway," Murphy said. A statement not a question.

"Because she's something special," I explained, looking at her, wishing I could take her back into my arms.

"Yes, she is," Garrett said, reaching up to cup Leigh's cheek. "But honest to God, Leigh. How could you let this happen? You have such a bright future ahead of you." He glanced at me. "If Nick's not the father, who is?"

"For right now, that doesn't matter, Dad."

"It most certainly does matter," Garrett said boldly, his cardiac episode apparently over. "The father has responsibilities. You'll need to get married."

The thought of Leigh with any other man filled me with a jealous rage.

Leigh looked pale.

Needing to take care of her, I opened some cabinets, found a glass and filled it with the iced tea I found in the refrigerator. Then I carried it over to where she stood. "Come on." I put my free hand on her low back and guided her to the chair next to her dad. "Sit down before you fall down."

She did. After a few sips, she turned to face her father. "I made a mistake, and now I'm pregnant. I won't compound that mistake by marrying a man I don't love and who doesn't love me."

"Don't be ridiculous," Garrett said, as if marrying for love was a farce.

"I've already decided," Leigh said. "I'm going to do this on my own."

"Leigh," Garrett said miserably.

"Not really on my own because I have you." She placed her hand on her father's knee. He covered it with his. "Even though I know you're disappointed in me right now, and you have every right to be, I know you'll always be there for me and my baby. You'll be a wonderful grandfather, like your father was a wonderful grandfather to me."

Tears leaked out of her eyes and down her cheeks. Damn if tears didn't fill Garrett's eyes, too. And mine. I glanced to my side, and added Murphy's to the list.

"You have me, too." The words popped out of my mouth without a second thought.

"And me." Murphy stepped forward.

"We could get married," tumbled out of my mouth.

Leigh looked at me like I had a trout flopping around on my head.

Chapter Fourteen

Leigh

Oh. My. God.

Nick did *not* just propose.

"Okay," he said, looking directly at me. "I know." He ran his hand over his head. "As far as marriage proposals go, that one sucked. I mean, I don't even have a ring."

"You could use this one." Murphy pulled on a chain around his neck to reveal two silver colored rings dangling on the end. "They belonged to my Lilly." He held them out to me. "She'd love for you to have them."

"I…" didn't know what to say. Emotion clogged my throat.

Nick walked toward me, taking my hands into his, staring into my eyes. "I know we've only known each other for a few weeks, but it's been long enough for me to know you're the one for me, Leigh."

So sincere, but, "Do you love me?" I refused to marry for any reason but love.

Nick hesitated, and I had my answer. I tried to pull my hands away, but he wouldn't let me.

"Yes," he said. "I do love you."

If he did, then why hadn't he said so before today? "No, you don't."

"I do," he said calmly.

"You hesitated."

"Because before I said those words, which I have never said to another woman, I'll have you know, I wanted to be sure I meant them. It took me a few seconds to be absolutely, positively sure that yes, I do love you. That I want us to be together."

He couldn't possibly love me. "It's too soon. And the baby, I don't expect you to—"

"I love you and I'll love your baby…like it was my own."

"You don't want children. They ruin everything, you said so yourself."

"I don't want *obnoxious* children who say rude things. We'll have to raise our child better than that."

Our child? Everything was happening too fast…so unexpected. He sounded sincere and sweet, but I couldn't take a chance, wouldn't tie him down.

I walked over to Murphy. "Thank you for offering, but no." I took the rings from his hand and tucked them back beneath his shirt.

Nick said, "If you want something different, we can go shopping. You can pick out whatever you want."

I gave Murphy a kiss on the cheek. "It would be an honor

to wear your wonderful Lilly's rings," I told him, adding, "Someday. But not today."

I turned to Nick. "Thank you for offering." I walked to him and gave him a hug. "But, no." I stepped back to look up at him. "I won't rush into marriage because I'm scared of the future. And I won't let you rush into marriage because you're trying to be honorable or because you feel sorry for me."

"I don't—"

"If you'd like for us to continue dating after the summer, I would like that." I gave him a small smile. "Very much."

"I do want to."

Pure joy surged inside of me. "After the baby's born, if we're still together, and you still want to, we can talk about marriage."

He pulled me into his arms. "I'll still want to."

I hoped so.

"What about your job?" my dad asked me.

I let out a breath and stepped away from the safety of Nick's embrace. Over the past forty-eight hours I'd given it a lot of thought. "I'll call them tomorrow and tell them I can't accept it."

"Damn it." He pushed up from his chair.

"Please, Dad." I set my hand on his shoulder. "Calm down. I'll find something else. Something local that won't require such long hours and so much travel." I looked up into the eyes of the man who'd raised me. "You taught me to work hard and be self-sufficient. I'll make you proud. I promise."

Dad softened in an instant. "You've always made me proud, Leigh. I love you."

I threw my arms around him. "I love you, too." He gave me a tight squeeze back.

When he stepped away, he pointed directly at Nick. "Now you. Why haven't you responded to my job offer?"

Nick stared right back at him, standing tall, not the least bit intimidated. Good for him! "I wasn't sure if you made your very generous offer based on my skills and experience or based on my relationship with your daughter."

Dad nodded approvingly. "A little of both." He sat back down. "Your relationship with my daughter is what got you in the door. But your resumé, your interview, and an exceptional reference from your last supervisor are what earned you the job offer."

"Good to know," Nick said.

"So you'll take it?" Dad asked.

Nick looked at me. "Leigh and I will discuss it."

"As long as you know," Dad said to Nick, "I will not stand for my future son-in-law, especially one with your credentials, working for anyone but me."

What? "Dad! Nick is not your future-son-in-law."

"But someday soon I'd like to be," Nick said, looking at me. "And I think it needs to be said that I love you for you, Leigh, not for who your dad is or for the lucrative job he offered me."

"I know that, Nick." Without a doubt.

"I'm a hard-worker and self-sufficient, too."

"Yes he is," Murphy added.

"As of yesterday I've got three job offers for us to talk over."

I loved that he valued my opinion.

"Wait a minute," my dad said.

"Stop it, Dad. Nick will decide which job he's going to take." Hopefully it'd be the job with The DeGray Fund. My dad needed someone like Nick on his staff, and he'd always said he wanted to keep his company in the family.

Murphy walked over to stand beside me. "You remind me of my Lilly. It only took me one date to know she was the one for me. My son? Met his wife and married her six weeks later. They're happily married to this day." He glanced over at Nick, then back at me. "We Kenzy men don't fool around when the right woman comes along."

"No, we don't," Nick said, looking down at me, his eyes filled with affection. "Which is why, when you're ready, I'd love for you to be my wife, for us to raise your baby as our baby."

My love for Nick swelled in my chest, and I realized, that even though I felt it, I'd never said the words. So I did. "I love you, too, you know."

"I know." He pulled me into his arms. "I see it in your eyes. I hear it in your voice. I feel it in your touch."

I hugged him tight, feeling blessed to have found such a wonderful man.

"Now that that's settled," my dad said, "let's set a date."

"No," I told him firmly. "Not until after the baby's born. Not until Nick sees what life will be like with a newborn and he's sure he wants to take on a new baby and a wife at the same time.

"I will," he said quietly.

Time would tell.

Epilogue

Nick
Four months later

"What's all this?" Leigh asked, looking toward the dining room as she walked over to give me a kiss. Since the summer, we'd been splitting our time between her dad's house, my granddad's house, and my apartment. Tonight I wanted her all to myself, so we were spending the night in the city.

I swiveled around and pulled her body to mine. "How was your day?" Turned out Hollis and Hamilton knew an exceptional employee when they interviewed one. Rather than accepting Leigh's resignation before she'd even started, they'd offered to modify her job to include only local travel when absolutely necessary. After the baby was born, she'd be job-sharing with another woman who was currently on maternity leave.

Leigh smiled. "Good. How was yours?"

Work at The DeGray Group was high-pressure and

exhausting, and I loved every minute of it. "Good." Today, with her father's blessing, I'd left work early to come home to prepare a special dinner. Not that I'd cooked, mind you. But I'd done everything else: flowers, candles, and non-alcoholic bubbly. I'd set a damn nice table, too, if I did say so myself.

"You used my mom's china," Leigh noticed.

I'd also used Grandma Lilly's crystal glasses that Murphy had insisted I take after Leigh had commented on how beautiful they were.

Speaking of beautiful. "You're looking exceptionally beautiful today," in a dark blue pant suit with her hair up in a bun, her feet bare, and her toenails painted a pretty peach color.

She set her hands at her low back, stuck out her round belly, and said, "I'm looking exceptionally pregnant today."

"Beautifully pregnant." I compromised, because she was. "How's our baby girl?" I rubbed her belly. As soon as we'd found out we were having a girl, we'd decided on the name Lilly Rose – Lilly for my grandma, and Rose for Leigh's mom.

"She doesn't like the chicken salad at the deli down the street from my office."

For the last month Leigh had been having terrible problems with indigestion.

"How does she feel about chicken piccata from La Mondas?"

"Oh." Leigh smiled. "We love chicken piccata from La Mondas!" She walked into the dining room. "But why so fancy? What's the occasion?"

The doorbell rang.

I paid the delivery man and carried dinner to the table.

"The occasion is," I began unpacking the box, "I love you."

While that was true, it wasn't the only reason I'd planned a special dinner.

Leigh stepped up to help me, placing the bread in the basket and plating my meal while I served up hers. "I love you, too," she said, glancing at me from the corners of her eyes.

All the food put out, I carried the empty containers into the kitchen. "Sit down," I yelled. "I'll be there in a minute." I slid my hand into the pocket of my dress pants, palming the velvet ring box I'd been carrying around with me since picking it up at the jewelers that afternoon.

Tonight had been set in motion three months ago, when Leigh had finally contacted the biological father of her baby. At her request, I'd accompanied them to dinner. The moment that stupid man happily, and with equal parts relief and appreciation, agreed to waive all paternal rights, Leigh's baby had become our baby. And I'd decided, right then and there, that I didn't want to wait any longer than absolutely necessary to make them both mine…officially.

With Leigh's many thoughtful gestures, she made me feel happy and loved. With her little touches, she'd turned my functional apartment into a warm, inviting home I looked forward to returning to each night, especially when I knew she'd be joining me there. I loved her with all of my heart, and while I knew she loved me, too, I had no idea how she'd respond to my proposal.

I inhaled a fortifying breath, wishing I hadn't agreed to give up alcohol for the duration of her pregnancy.

In the dining room I found Leigh seated at the table with her napkin in her lap, waiting for me. Without wasting anymore time, I went right over to her and got down on one knee. She started to say something, but I wouldn't let her finish. "I know we agreed to hold off on discussing marriage until after the baby is born." I took her left hand in mine as I removed the ring from my pocket with my free hand. "But I've changed my mind."

I looked up into her eyes. The love I saw there gave me the courage to go on. "I love you, Leigh. And I don't want to wait."

"But—"

"Do you love me?"

"You know I do."

"Enough to marry me?"

Tears pooled in her eyes. She nodded. "But—"

"I promise to be a loving husband and father."

She sniffled.

"I promise to do my absolute best to be a good provider and take care of you and our daughter and any other children we're blessed with."

"I know you will," she said.

"So will you marry me? Sooner rather than later?"

She hesitated, and I prepared to start my speech to convince her.

But then she nodded, and my heart almost exploded with happiness as I slid the ring onto her finger.

"It's beautiful," she said, holding up her hand to look at it.

"Storme helped me pick out the setting. The diamond came from your mother's engagement ring, not because I couldn't afford one, but because your father offered, and we both thought it'd make the ring extra special."

Leigh started to cry.

"Ah, honey." I helped her to stand and took her into my arms. "Don't cry."

"They're happy tears. I love you so much." She kissed my cheek. "Thank you for finding me at the bonfire and for inviting me to Murphy's house for a barbecue. And thank you for not running away when I told you about my…situation."

"I will never run away from you," I assured her, leaning back so I could look her directly in the eyes as I placed a hand on her belly. "We're in this together. Forever."

The End

Thank you for taking the time to read **Summer Temptation**. If you enjoyed it, please consider telling your friends or posting a short review. Word of mouth is an author's best friend and much appreciated.

And don't forget to check out the rest of the Hot in the Hamptons series with **Summer Dreaming** (Kelsey's story) by Liz Matis and **Summer Sins** (Storme's story) by Jennifer Probst!

Keep the burn going with the next 2 books in the Hot in the Hamptons series…

Summer Dreaming
By: Liz Matis

I'm looking for a hero. Not.

You'd think as a new college grad I'd be looking for the perfect job and the perfect man. Well, I'm not. Summer is here and instead of plotting my future, I'm playing in the Hamptons with my two best friends. Sun and sex is all I'm looking for. Then I meet Sean Dempsey, my fantasy lifeguard in the flesh. But he is more than just a hot bod with a whistle. And after he makes a daring save, I'm thinking a hero is exactly what I've been looking for all along.

To the rescue…

By day I guard the beaches in the Hamptons, by night I've had my fair share of summer flings. Then I meet Kelsey Mitchell, a girl with eyes like the setting sun and I burn for more. Something I have no right to ask of her…forever.

Summer Sins

By: Jennifer Probst

Summer fun before my wedding...

I have one goal this summer. Hang with my besties for some much needed sun, sand, and relaxation while I put the final touches on my idyllic wedding. I didn't count on meeting a smart-mouthed, bad boy biker whose gaze burns hotter than a beach bonfire. I never planned to lose myself, body and soul, and question my entire future. Now, I have to make a choice that's tearing me apart, and could shatter the lives of the two men I love...

Turns into summer sins....

I have one goal this summer. CHILL. Do nothing. Nada. I need simple before I have to head into Manhattan to take on a high powered position on Wall Street. I didn't count on a dark haired, inky- eyed spitfire who'd spin my world upside down, or make me burn for things I never thought I wanted. I vowed to make her my summer fling, but had no idea she was claimed by another. And now that she possessed not only my body but my soul, the stakes are too high for me to lose her...

About the Author

Wendy S. Marcus is an award-winning author of contemporary romance. A nurse by trade, Wendy holds a Master of Science in Health Care Administration, a degree that does her absolutely no good as she now spends her days, nights, and weekends mucking around in her characters' lives creating conflict, emotion, and, of course, a happily ever after. Wendy lives in the beautiful Hudson Valley region of New York. To learn more visit her website: http://www.WendySMarcus.com.

Also by WENDY S. MARCUS

Random House Loveswept Contemporary Romances

Loving You Is Easy **(Loving You #1)**

She's a survivor of the front lines of politics. He's a wounded soldier returning home from the battlefield. Can they place their trust in the power of love? Nobody plays the role of perfect politician›s daughter better than quiet, respectable math teacher Brooke Ellstein. But she won't be caught swimming with the sharks again, not after the son of a wealthy donor sinks his teeth into her and gets away with it. Still, political connections have their perks, such as heading up the governor's "Support Our Troops" pen-pal initiative--and getting first dibs on the smoking-hot sergeant whose picture shakes her right down to her goody-two-shoes. When corresponding with sweet, classy Brooke, Shane Develen instinctively hides his commando tattoos and blue-collar roots--and he can tell that she's hiding something, too. But Shane knows he's gained her trust when Brooke gives him a blisteringly sexy photo. Then he's injured in an ambush and a fellow soldier posts the snapshot online. Overnight, Brooke's reputation turns to ashes. Even though he's totally wrong for her, Shane shows up on Brooke's doorstep, determined to set things right--and discovers that right or wrong has nothing on the chemistry they share.

***All I Need Is You* (Loving You #2) Coming October 6, 2015**

Perfect for fans of Kristan Higgins and Robyn Carr, this sexy yet sweet military romance reunites a headstrong dancer and a rugged army soldier after one steamy encounter tears them apart. As a dancer who creates mesmerizing visions onstage, Neve James is looking for the same kind of stability in her love life. Her pen pal, Rory McRoy, is on leave from deployment in Afghanistan, so she heads to Boston to surprise him. After corresponding for months as part of a "Support Our Troops" initiative—and exchanging dozens of "Read When You're Alone" letters—Neve knows what Rory likes, and she intends to fulfill his every fantasy. But all they get are a few blissful moments together before they're interrupted by a woman claiming to be Rory's fiancée. Rory has fallen hard for Neve's letters. When he finally meets her in person, he has to have her, right then and there—until Neve takes off in a fit of anger. Forced to return to Afghanistan before he can fix things between them, Rory waits four agonizing months to prove that he's not the man Neve thinks he is. But by the time he arrives in New York, she's already made up her mind. Luckily, Rory never backs down from a challenge, and he's prepared to put everything on the line for love.

Cosmopolitan Red Hot Reads From Harlequin

***The V-Spot* (a novella)**

How hot is your night going to get? Take the quiz and find out!

1. You're a curvy, cute and practical nurse, ready to unleash your inner naughty nymphette for your 25th birthday. You start with...

a. Chocolate cake.

b. Champagne. Lots of it.

c. A blind date set up by your daring best friend.

2. Your guy turns out to be popular (and insanely hot) wrestler Brody "The Bull" Bullock. You...

a. Run for the door.

b. Admire his hotness, then run for the door.

c. Imagine him naked.

3. You're meeting Brody at The V-Spot, a "Voyeur Motel." What are you wearing?

a. A cute sundress with wedge sandals

b. You're not going anywhere without Spanx

c. Doesn't matter. Brody is sexy enough that it's all coming off!

If you selected all of the above, you're in for the night of your life....